Ghost Stories

By Hank Roberts

Edited by Philip Levin
Published by Doctor's Dreams
PO Box 4808
Biloxi, MS 39535
www.Doctors-Dreams.com
writerpllevin@gmail.com

ISBN: 978-1-942181-27-9

Prepared in the United States of America

Ghost Stories contains three novellas by retired dentist Hank Roberts. The first two are the two volume previously published books "The Mysterious Mansion" and "The Mysterious Mansion Part Two." These books tell of a twenty-first century couple who buy a haunted mansion in Alabama and have to discover who are the ghosts haunting it and how to lay them to rest. The third book, "Tales of Uncle Frank," is a never before published novella set in the beginning of the twentieth century of four teenage boys and their interaction with an old woodman hermit who tells ghost stories and leads them on scary adventures.

The Mysterious Mansion

A Ghost Story

By Hank Roberts

Edited by Philip Levin

Book One: The Mysterious Mansion

Book One: The Mysterious Mansion

Prologue

The old man's death in 1975 was shrouded with mystery. Except for his youth spent abroad, his entire life had been lived as a hermit, holed up in his antebellum birth home. When the police entered his house to investigate his death, they found his crumpled body dressed in regular bedclothing in a large overstuffed chair in his bedroom. Although the man had only been dead a few days, the chair in which he sat, along with all the furniture in the entire house, were covered with spider webs and dust. After the coroner removed the body, the mansion, along with the associated small gated yard, was locked. No one ever again had the nerve to venture inside.

Chapter 1

Marley Robbins stood outside the brick windowless building with the sign, "Station 47," hanging above the door. He pushed down the bit of anxiety, concentrating on the exhilaration of finally having the first step in his newscasting career. Checking his watch, he waited until the second hand reached the top, so that at exactly two o'clock he rang the studio's doorbell.

A minute passed.

He turned to look at a woman walking by pushing a stroller. He gave her a smile and a wave and was pleased when she returned them both. Small town friendliness, he decided.

He was about to press the bell again when the door opened to reveal a mid-height, fat balding man wearing an open collared shirt with food stains.

Marley held out his hand. "Uh. Mr. Chester Cohen?"

The fat man engulfed Marley's hand with his own, shaking it vigorously. "Yep, yep. You bet! You must be Marvin Roberts."

"Uh, Marley Robbins. You, uh, told me to be here at two, right?"

Chester checked his watch. "Punctual, huh? I like that in an employee. Yep, yep. Sure do.

Well, come on in, young fellow. Follow me to my little office and we can talk."

Marley stepped in, surveying the filming studio they passed through. It had three cameras set up facing a green screen background, with a couple of chairs and other props scattered around the floor space. They entered Chester's office, a space mostly filled by a small desk and a couple of plastic chairs. On top of a file cabinet a black tabby stared down at Marley.

Chester settled in the chair behind his desk. "Have a seat, have a seat."

Marley saw that both chairs overflowed with stacks of paper, so he remained standing.

Chester reached up and scratched the sweat spot under his left armpit. "Glad you could come be a part of Station 47, Mr. Roberts. I loved your resumé. Checked out all your YouTube videos, too. Say, you want to know what made me decide to hire you?"

Marley, who had been studying the way Chester picked his nose while he talked, realized he hadn't been paying attention. He reran what he had heard the man say and replied, "Yes, sir. What made you hire me?"

"Your YouTube video about that cat farm." Chester pointed at his cat. "I liked your style – homey – local. I think a report like that every now and then will really catch on here in Greenwell."

"Thank you, Mr. Cohen. I hope I'll please you. By the way, how's your gout?"

"Gout?" Mr. Cohen cocked one eyebrow. "How did you know I have gout?"

Marley nodded at Chester's hand. "It shows in the knuckles, you know. Also," he pointed to under one of the chairs, "I saw the slippers with one toe cut out."

Mr. Cohen chortled. "Ha! You're a bright one, aren't you? You can call me Chester. Come along, fellow. I'll introduce you to your co-worker. She's the one that makes the studio work, so you better get along with her."

The walked out of the manager's office, back through the studio, and into the production chamber, a darkened room with three computer monitors running. On the wall four muted television screens showed various channels.

"Allie Burton, I'd like you to meet Marty Roberts. He's the newscaster I just hired."

Marley watched her peek up from around her computer screen. Limp brown hair framed her freckled cheeks. She wore no makeup, and the computer screen glow made her face seem pale, even ghostly. He immediately fell in love with that face.

He held out his hand. "I'm Marley Robbins. Is it Allie?"

She pushed back her chair and took his hand with her own limp grip. "Yes, Allison Burton. Everyone calls me Allie. I do the production here at Station 47. I ... uh, I ..."

Marley watched Allie's face flush and she abruptly sat down, hiding behind the computer screen.

Marley stepped back. "Sorry about what?"

Mr. Cohen's large pot belly shook with his chuckle. "Allie's a bit shy, but she's good at her job. Been with me the whole six months I've owned and run this station."

"Well that's my ambition," Marley replied. "I'm going to be good at my job too." He leaned over the screen so he could see Allie, who looked up hesitantly at his attempt at a reassuring smile. "I'm sure we'll get along just fine," he insisted.

Mr. Cohen told Marley that the station didn't make a lot of money, so he'd only be paying him for three hours a day, Monday through Friday. His first responsibility would be to prepare weather reports each morning. Allie would film him and then broadcast them throughout the day, in between the old movies and sit coms that made up the station's general venue.

"After you get your feet wet, I'd like you to start doing some local features, like that cat thingy you did. Maybe we can work up to a full half hour slot in the evenings. You'll be responsible for obtaining material for your show, and you'll have to run it by me first. Okay. Any questions?"

Marley shook his head.

"Good, good. I'll see you first thing tomorrow morning. Allie, why don't you take Marvin next door to Mabel's and give him some insight into our town?"

Mr. Cohen lumbered back into his office, and Marley stood looking down on the seated production woman. "Well? Coffee at Mabel's?"

Allie shook her head without looking up.

"Oh, come on. I just stepped off the Greyhound an hour ago and walked the three blocks to get here. If I'm going to be a reporter for Greenwell, Alabama, I need you to give me some ins and outs about life in this dusty old berg."

Again, she shook her head no.

He reached past her and picked up a book from her desk. He read the title out loud, "*The Rise and Fall of the Confederacy* by Jefferson Davis. Really? I loved this one. You can't beat a firsthand report for authenticity, even if it is a one-sided view."

Allie lifted her eyes to stare at him, perhaps the first prolonged eye contact she'd had with any man other than her father in several years. "You … you like history?"

"Oh yeah. Journalism was my major at Mississippi State, but I minored in history. I have a special yen for Civil War History."

She looked down at the book again, shuffling her feet. After a moment she looked back into his eyes. "Okay, then. Let's go get some coffee."

Mabel's Diner had that old-fashioned look, red and white checkered tiles and silver rimmed barstools. Allie led them to the furthest back booth where they settled on either side of the table. Marley gave the place his usual concentrated scan.

"Used to sell milkshakes and cigarcttcs, huh? I wonder what happened to the local paper?"

Allie threw him a questioning glance. "Sounds like you've done your Greenwell research."

"Not much. I just noticed the blenders gathering dust on a top shelf, so figured they used to be an item here, but not for several months at least. And there's an old advertisement for Chesterfield embossed on the window."

"That's right on," Allie said. "And how did you know the newspaper went out of business six years ago?"

Marley pointed to a series of small frames on the far wall. "There are awards for best restaurant in town and other local write-ups over there, but the last one is from several years ago, judging by the yellowing of the paper."

Mabel strolled up, a plaid apron across her generous belly and a steaming coffee pot in her right hand. Receiving nods from both Allie and Marley, she turned the two cups upright on the table and filled them. She glanced at Allie and gave Marley more than a once-over.

"You new in town?" she asked.

He stood and offered her a hand, then embarrassedly dropped it seeing as how she couldn't take it due to holding the coffee pot. "Uh, yes ma'am. My name's Marley Robbins. I've just gotten the position as head newscaster at Station 47 next door. I'm going to be an investigative reporter."

Mabel put her head back and let loose a roar of laughter. "Oh, that's rich, that's rich. 'Head newscaster' at that rinky-dink two-bit station, huh? Quite a big title. And 'investigative reporter?' This I gotta see." She laughed again. "What're you gonna investigate? Lost cats?" Indicating his dining companion with a toss of her head, "I was wondering what kind of fellow Allie would bring into my diner. A fellow dweeb. That's great." She put the coffee pot down on the table in order to wipe the tears from her eyes. After a minute of composing herself she asked,

"You two want anything besides coffee? I got some fresh peach pie."

Allie nodded vigorously. She informed Marley that Mabel's pie was renowned throughout the state, and then told Mable to bring them each a slice à la mode. The waitress left still chuckling.

Marley reached up and scratched behind his ear, muffing up the hair there so his silhouette now looked uneven, flat hair behind his left ear, exploded behind the right. "So. Greenwell, huh? What's it like?"

Allie thought through that question. "What have you heard?"

"Just what I could find on the Internet. Population 12,000 or so. Town itself is named after the Greenwell family, specifically Thomas Greenwell who founded it about 1840 to service his big cotton plantation. After the War Between the States, his son Daniel was a big benefactor of the town. I think there's a statue to him somewhere."

"Yes, right in front of town hall."

"Oh yeah, I saw that on my walk over. Didn't have time to read the inscription. Saw the War memorials around the courthouse too. Lots of history here I imagine."

He noticed Allie staring at him.

"What?"

"You said at the office you were going to be good at your job," she said. "And I was impressed with what you saw in this place. Would you mind if I gave you a little test?"

He carefully set his cup down in the middle of the saucer. "Test? What kind of test?"

She closed her eyes tightly and put her hands under the table.

"Marley, what color are my eyes?"

"They're brown with a touch of green."

She opened them up. "That's correct. And what jewelry am I wearing?"

He didn't hesitate. "You have a woven bracelet on your right wrist, one of those plastic MIA things on your left, and your right index finger holds a gold band with blue stones. In addition, of course, you have those gold loop earrings."

She nodded, bringing her hands back above the table to show him he had been exactly right. "You really do notice everything, don't you?"

"Well, maybe not everything – certainly about you, though."

She blushed and turned her face down.

"No. I didn't mean it that way." He ruffled the hairlock again. "I meant, that's what I do, you know. People I meet, I've trained myself to observe the details. Like Mabel. Did you notice she has a hearing aid in her left ear, and she's had breast cancer?"

Allie looked over at Mabel, who was coming towards them with two slices of pie, each topped with a scoop of ice cream melting into a tempting white pool in its plate. Staring, she tried to see if she could tell anything about the woman's chest.

Mable looked down at her blouse. "What, did I spill something?"

Allie shook her head. "No, no. I'm sorry. I was thinking of something else."

The waitress placed the pies down and returned to her counter.

"What did you see?" Marley asked Allie.

"Nothing. What did YOU see?"

"The left breast rides higher and seems a bit fuller. Either she had an implant or wears padding after having her breast removed."

"Couldn't she just have different size breasts?"

Marley shook his head. "Much less likely."

Allie shook her head in admiration. "A regular Sherlock Holmes, aren't you?" she said, with a strongly Southern drawled English accent.

Marley laughed. "Yes, I suppose so."

They worked on their pies in silence for a few minutes.

"Have you always wanted to be an investigative reporter?" Allie asked.

"Yeah, that's always been my dream." He gobbled down his pie and dribbled the ice cream puddle from the plate into his spoon, licking it clean. "Since I graduated from college last year, I've applied to fifty television stations across the country. This was the only offer I got. So … I guess I gotta make this one work. You know of any great town mysteries I can investigate?"

Allie put her fork down, interlocking her hands on the tabletop. "Now that you mention it, there is one great big one. You mentioned Thomas and Daniel Greenwell. Well, the original Greenwell mansion still exists. It's about a half-mile off the town square on its own separate hill."

Marley shrugged. "An old mansion, huh? Period pieces I suppose. What, they give tours?"

"Nope. No one's been inside it for over forty years since the last Greenwell died there."

"Yeah? Must be pretty dusty by now. So, what's the big mystery?"

She leaned forward to within a foot of his nose. In a barely audible whisper, she said, "It's haunted!"

Chapter 2

The next morning Marley showed up at ten, dressed in his suit jacket, white collared shirt, and narrow red tie. Allie took one look at him and a huge grin erupted across her face.

"Is that what you were planning on wearing on TV?"

Marley looked down at his outfit. "Uh. Yes, why?"

"Because this is Greenwell, Alabama, that's why. You gotta look the part. Come on. We'll get you some clothes at the Goodwill store down the block."

She led him out, and at the store bought him jeans, a T-shirt with "Mabel's Diner" emblazoned across the front, and a cap featuring Greenwell's city seal prominently displayed.

Back in the studio, she showed him how to retrieve the weather report from the Internet and he wrote up copy for her to put on the teleprompter. What with equipment issues and rehearsals, it took them until one o'clock to get two weather reports filmed. Afterwards they walked next door to Mabel's for a rerun of coffee and peach pie.

"I'm super excited about your idea of my doing an investigative report on the Greenwell mansion," Marley said. "You gonna help me?"

She gave him a shy smile. "I think I could be talked into it."

Together they sketched out in his notebook the places they'd research for information about the family and the mansion. He said he'd go through all the local, county, and state records. She chose to research the local newspaper archives and the library.

Over the next two weeks, this is the story they put together.

Chapter 3

Thomas Greenwell came to this part of Alabama from Virginia in 1832. Although his age was uncertain, he probably was in his early twenties at the time. He'd brought his wife with him, a woman named Sarah. Within a month of his arrival, he'd bought 1,000 acres and by 1835 had built the family mansion. Within a few years he'd purchased another 10,000 acres, creating a huge plantation where the main cash crop was cotton.

In order for the family to produce and take to market such a large volume of cotton, Thomas Greenwell depended on a massive workforce of slaves. Traveling to New Orleans every other month, Mr. Thomas, as he was known, bought anywhere between eight and fifteen slaves each trip. The sources suggested he treated them harshly, but details on that were few. On the way back he'd sell about half of what he'd purchased to local farmers, making up for all the expenses of his trip.

He was a shrewd businessman. His cotton business thrived in the pre-Civil War days, as well as several side businesses, such as brick making and raising trophy horses. The plantation consisted of slave houses, stables, and specialty shops, including a blacksmith and coopery. He even had a special building where he would take a favorite female slave of the month, a place that earned the nickname, "Uncle Tom's Cabin."

Thomas Greenwell amassed a large fortune. With their great wealth and plentiful slave labor, the Greenwell mansion became renowned for hosting festive parties. There, the other area white planters would gather for cocktails on the veranda, discuss politics, and discuss the future of cotton and the nation.

The War Between the States changed all of the South, including the Greenwells. Thomas Greenwell enlisted immediately, rising to the rank of Colonel during the war, and dying in battle at the siege of Vicksburg. Thomas' two sons chose different sides, Daniel, eighteen-years-old, joined the Confederacy while his year-younger brother, Bobby, went north. Bobby was highly decorated, though Daniel not so much, around whom rumors swirled that he'd returned home with a fortune.

After the war, the two brothers tried to continue making the plantation work, despite the labor issues caused by the emancipation of their slaves. They disagreed about almost everything, especially the treatment of their workers. Daniel wanted the South to remain as it was and to hell with the new laws: paying workers pennies, requiring long hours of backbreaking labor, and enforcing compliance with the occasional whipping. Bobby took a more sympathetic tone, wanting to upgrade the prior slave quarters to provide decent housing for the workers and give them adequate salaries and working conditions. The townsfolk wrote about the angry arguments the brothers had, often in public such as at church or in a town store. No longer were there parties at the mansion.

One weekend, Daniel ordered all the servants to stay away from the house for the next three days. When they returned, there was no sign of Bobby. Daniel claimed his brother had taken his Union uniform and his sword and rode off. No one heard a word from him ever again.

Daniel sold about half of his land and helped promote the town. The soil was fertile, and with a few small industries set up on the river, including a cotton mill and a machinery shop, the town thrived. Daniel donated funds to further the town's prosperity, including building the town hall and library.

Daniel never married. Records showed that in 1890 at the age of 47 he adopted a newborn baby. The birth certificate had been lost, but there had been a brief report about the birth of Nathan Greenwell in the local paper. No pictures of him could be found. Nathan was sent to Europe as an infant where he was raised by private nannies, and then attended a small private school. He studied at the Sorbonne, earning a degree in liberal arts. One source suggested he traveled around Europe studying the occult. After his father's death in 1922, he returned to the plantation, though he was never actually seen to arrive. Once he entered the old mansion, he never set foot out of it again.

Nathan had a tall brick fence built around the mansion and a small piece of the yard surrounding it. He kept the twenty acres of the forest on the hill where his home stood and sold off all the remaining land. Through the next thirty years, his only contact with any human was an African American man who served as manservant. After he died in the 1950s, Nathan spent the rest of his life in isolation. He had his food and needed supplies delivered to his home's porch, with his trust fund at the bank paying all charges. Occasional strange bulky packages came with foreign stamps, adding to the mysteries of Nathan's reclusiveness.

For the next few years after his death the mansion grounds outside the wall became a hangout for teenagers or secret lovers. Sometimes these night visitors reported seeing a candle flickering in an upstairs window. They'd report seeing someone's shadow on the shade, crossing the room or sitting in a rocking chair. At times strange noises filtered out: howls, moans, and piteous cries. In the winter, smoke billowed from the tall chimney, although no one had been in the house to light a fire. After enough of these occurrences, almost no one dared to get anywhere near the place, especially at night.

Chapter 4

"So, what do you think?" Marley asked, after they reviewed the history they'd gathered. "Should we go investigate the Greenwell mansion this weekend?"

Allie froze, her cup halfway to her mouth. "You mean … actually go IN there?"

"Yes. That's exactly what I mean. Don't tell me you believe all those ghost tales I've been reporting on the evening news."

"Oh, of course not." Allie tried to smile, but couldn't get her lips to turn up. "Well, maybe a little."

Marley watched her hand shake so much she began spilling coffee over the rim and onto Mabel's paper placemat. She set her cup down in a small brown puddle she'd made.

"Really?" he asked, his eyebrows raised.

"Yes! I'm scared to death of ghosts. While I'd absolutely love to go explore the history and artifacts there, I'm not going inside that old mansion as long as it's haunted. If you want to go, I'll drive you up and wait outside. You'll want to do it during full sunlight of course."

He reached and ruffed up that hairlock again. "No, I don't think so. This adventure definitely calls for a night visit. I'll bring a sleeping bag, a bit of food and water, and some supplies. I'm eager to see just what this ghost has to say."

Allie shook her head, and then reached up and stroked his cheek, the first time she'd touched him since that first handshake. "You must be the bravest man I've ever met."

Saturday afternoon, Allie drove Marley to the foot of the Greenwell mansion. Besides energy bars and colas, he'd brought a flashlight, bug spray, notepad, Swiss-pocketknife, and a sleeping bag. He told Allie he would prove there wasn't any ghost, just a creaky old mansion.

The lock and chains securing the heavy iron gate had rusted from the weather and crumbled at Marley's touch. He pushed and the gate swung open with an eerie squeal. Inside, the grounds were a jungle of weeds growing to about six feet, just low enough so that when he stepped into the courtyard he could see over them to get his first look at the house. He jumped when the gate slammed closed behind him.

The home, a two-story large-winged mansion, had the classic look of trim red bricks, white shutters, and a huge chimney coming out the center of the house. Vines encircled much of the building, though an upstairs window remained completely unobscured.

Beneath the thick vines and overgrowth, Marley could make out the outline of a walkway meandering through the courtyard towards the large front veranda. As he made his way along the path, he passed by several structures that he realized once had been beautiful fountains and planters. He imagined how elegant the mansion must have once been.

When he reached the front door, he reached up and used the ornate clapper to produce a loud, distinctive knock. The door creaked wide open, and for a moment Marley thought he saw a butler standing there, though the image dissipated in the blink of his eyes.

Marley cringed as a cloud of foul-smelling mildew struck his nose. He took two steps in, each one raising a cloud of dust, and stood, waiting for his eyes to fully adjust to the darkness. Pointing his flashlight, he found large pieces of furniture loomed like a foreboding forest: a tall mahogany chest, large end tables with antique lamps, and overstuffed armchairs. Spider webs and rodent droppings gave evidence to the identities of the current residents.

He walked over to the drapes, most of them moth and rat eaten, and with a swish opened them enough to let in some of the fading sunlight. He turned and his gaze fell onto two large oil paintings on the far wall. The first portrayed Thomas in all his grim glory, his black vested suit topped with a starched white shirt. In the second,

Daniel, in a frock coat with vest, stood before a portrayal of his statue in the town square.

Despite its current condition, there was still the appearance of this once being a home of great wealth and importance. Massive crystal chandeliers hung from sixteen-foot high ceilings. A beautifully carved wooden border ran along the walls' upper edges and he could make out remnants of lovely murals on the ceiling. On the walls hung portraits of massive landscapes depicting scenery that had once been the majestic Greenwell plantation. There were fields of cotton with slaves. There were pictures of men hunting quail and pheasant. There were forest scenes laced with large deer. Paintings of prize horses hung on both sides of the fireplace.

Marley's attention riveted on that fireplace, a massive structure at least twelve by five feet in opening and a good five or six feet deep. The mantle was constructed of the finest marble with the inside lined with bricks that each had the initials T.G embedded in them. There was a large iron grate within the concavity used to hold the logs to be burned. The size of the fireplace allowed for Marley to climb completely into its bowels. He noticed that a couple of the bricks in the back were loose. Taking these out, he discovered a small chamber hidden behind the hearth. Using his pocketknife to loosen the old plaster, he soon had made an opening large enough to squeeze inside.

The room stood about eight-foot square, with a ceiling so low Marley had to stoop to prevent bumping his head. His flashlight revealed the one item in the room, a six-foot long stone sarcophagus.

Thinking for a moment of curses he'd heard about old sarcophaguses, Marley's hands trembled as he moved the coffin's lid enough to train his light inside. It reflected back a sword handle resting on top of a white muslin cloth. Using his pocketknife to slash a six-inch hole, the drape parted to reveal beneath it a smiling skull.

Chapter 5

Marley closed the sarcophagus, squeezed out of the tomb, and replaced the bricks. Crawling out of the fireplace, Marley proceeded to explore the other rooms on the first floor. One small closet held an old toilet, the type with the reservoir box six feet above it.

Down a short hallway he entered the dining room, a space long enough to easily hold its huge mahogany table surrounded by two-dozen chairs. Along the wall, glass-doored cabinets showed rows and rows of serving ware. There were fine crystal glasses and coffee cups with gold rims. China dishes were neatly stacked and ready to serve some 25 people. In the drawers under the counter, Marley found sterling silver cutlery and serving utensils, along with at least 100 special serving pieces. All the silver was carefully stored in large wooden boxes lined with felt. Marley imagined the dinners served here, the guests in their nineteenth century antebellum finery, laughing and bragging of how the South would win the war.

Marley stepped over the broken door leading into the kitchen, finding the large room stocked with pieces from the 1920s: an old icebox, a tin barrel sink, and a wood-burning stove. The light fixture was electric, a bare-bulb socket with frayed wiring running across the ceiling and down the wall to an old push-button switch. He opened the grate covering the stove's belly and peaked inside, finding it empty.

Along an upper wall, shiny copper pots and pans hung on hooks, neatly arranged like soldiers ready for battle. Another wall held an array of knives, including cleavers, graters, santokus – all types and shapes to cut and chop with. There was one knife missing. Strangely, unlike everything else in the house, the pots and knives weren't covered in webs or dust. In fact, they seemed to gleam in the light coming through the window.

From the kitchen there was a backdoor which he unlatched and stepped through. Here he found a water pump with a large rusted galvanized trough, big enough to wash dishes or perhaps provide water for animals. A small stone walkway led through the weeds towards the back fence and he imagined that, a hundred and seventy years ago, meandered down to the slave quarters.

Returning to the living room, he inspected the antique stairway leading to the upper story. It had beautiful ornate banisters with steps covered with a dingy carpeting, full of dust and rat droppings. Marley noticed that there was no dust on the handrails. He stooped down to get a close look at the stairs and thought that he could make out a faint set of footprints going up. There were none coming down.

Ascending the steps, he stopped to study the collection of very old photographs and oil paintings of members of the Greenwell family along the walls, all mounted in ornate golden frames. About halfway up the staircase hung a Daguerrean photo of a middle-aged Thomas Greenwell, a woman who Marley presumed was Sarah Greenwell, and their two sons, looking to be young teenagers. Knowing their ages, Marley figured this had to be taken just before the Civil War, so between 1855 and 1858. He studied the faces, clothing, and stances, trying to figure out their personalities from their portraits. Daniel, on the far left, seemed separate, a bit aloof. Next came Thomas standing erect, a half smile on his face. Beside him, Sarah looked down upon her youngest son, as if casting a blessing upon him. Bobby, in his turn, held his mother's hand while he looked off to the left, as if something had caught his attention, or maybe in a daydream.

At the top of the stairs, Marley found a long hallway lined on both sides with doors. Behind the first door he found a large sitting room, complete with ashtrays and decayed cigars. A chess set with pieces neatly aligned sat in one corner, bookshelves full of mouse-eaten tomes made up two of the walls, and on either side of the single window hung oil paintings of Paris.

The next door opened into a bedroom with furnishings typical of the early nineteenth century, including a large double bed, armoire, chest of drawers, and two linen-covered dressing tables. Etched crystal containers with sterling silver lids on each table held various items, such as jewelry, dried powder, and combs. Hairbrushes and shaving equipment sat neatly aligned around a mirror. In the armoire he found a dozen women's dresses and a couple of suits, including the one Thomas wore in the downstairs painting. He closed the door of what he labeled Thomas and Sarah's room, and stepped across the hall to open the next door.

This one, another bedroom, had similar accoutrements as the first, though with only a single-sized bed and no jewelry. In the bottom drawer of the dresser he found a neatly folded Confederate Civil War uniform. "Daniel Greenwell's room," he muttered.

Next came a small office, hardly big enough for its magnificent rolltop desk and chair. Marley jimmied the lock with his pocketknife and rolled up the top. There he found a stack of yellow papers and a handful of old photographs. Hidden in the back of one drawer, Marley discovered a bag of coins in an old leather bag and a cedar box containing a few parchment papers with seals and stamps. He stuck the bag in his pocket and set the box on the floor of the hallway outside the door.

The next door opened into a more modernized bedroom, furnishing more typical of the 1950s, including a radio and a big box television. This and the office had been wired for electricity, and, unlike the other bedrooms, a closet had been constructed in one corner, its door secured with a strong lock. Here, beside the bed and dresser, sat a large overstuffed chair. Marley realized that this chair matched the description the police reported as where Nathan had been found dead. A tremble went through Marley as he imagined Nathan sitting there, night after night, reading by the lamp beside the chair. There was even a book on the little table.

On a shelf above the bed a row of strange looking objects attracted Marley's attention. He picked up the first object, a plastic bag that disintegrated in his hand, tumbling its contents of square gray tiles. Each had a different strange symbol on it. Next to it was a Ouija Board snuggling next to a gray metal sphere. Other objects included a pendulum, a voodoo doll, and several more he didn't recognize.

Shutting the door on the last Greenwell's death chamber, Marley continued his journey, opening the next door to find a pink tiled bathroom with porcelains from the 1940s, including toilet, sink, and claw-footed bathtub. His opening of the door stirred up a layer of dust that danced before the sunset beam coming in through the soda-bottle glass.

He reached the final doorway and paused, surveying what he'd passed. There'd been rooms for Thomas, Daniel, and Nathan. That only left Bobby. When he touched the doorknob, an electric shock traveled through his body and he imagined he heard a loud scream coming from downstairs. The door was locked, and no turning of the knob or pushing on the boards let him into that room.

Chapter 6

Dusk had fallen, and back downstairs he found that the light coming in through the dilapidated curtains provided barely any illumination. Pushing the grate out of the way, he laid his sleeping bag out on the bed of the fireplace and applied the insect spray around the hearth's opening to keep out the night bugs and rodents. Laying his head down on his backpack, he soon fell sound asleep.

Marley startled awake to a strange howling sound. Checking his watch, he read a few minutes before midnight. He crawled out of his bag and flipped on his flashlight, watching a rat and a half dozen cockroaches scurry away. Following the howl towards the kitchen, he discovered the noise came from the grate he'd left open on the stove, allowing air to rush in and cause the strange noise. He latched it shut and headed back to his bed.

He'd just settled deep into his sleeping bag again when he heard a clattering coming from the kitchen. He made his way back in and flashed his light on the cooking pans. Several of them were swinging gently and one hook was empty. Sweeping the light on the floor, he discovered the missing pan on the floor. Picking it up, he found that it had a huge dent right in the middle of it.

Marley placed the dented pan on the counter and swept his light around, landing it on the knife rack. There he realized another knife was missing, a large cleaver, the type of tool used to chop through bone. Marley grabbed one of the other large knives for his own use, just in case, and headed back to his bed.

He'd just gotten back into his sleeping bag when he heard the sound of someone walking across the solid wooden floors above him.

He crawled out of bed, grabbing his flashlight in one hand and the knife in the other, and clumped up the stairs. Halfway up he called out, "Whoever's there, you better not cause any trouble. I'm armed."

He reached the top of the stairs just in time to see a flickering light go into the bedroom at the far end of the hall. Hurrying down the hallway, he was surprised to find this last door which had been securely locked was now partially open.

"Hello?" he called, letting the silence extend for a minute before pushing the door open the rest of the way. His flashlight showed him a bedroom similar to the one he'd labeled Daniel's. A single bed, armoire, and dresser. He took a step in and stood, pointing his flashlight in various corners.

For a moment Marley felt dizzy. He blinked, and when he opened his eyes the room had changed. It was now clean and bright, oil lamps burning and a clean breeze drifting in through the window, its bright curtains fluttering. A young man sat on the small dressing chair, a black man combing his hair.

The man stood and he and the servant walked right through Marley, creating a chill through his body, and continued out the door. Marley followed them and watched them drift through the bathroom door. When Marley stepped in, he found the room empty, but water was dripping and the tiles gleamed from the light above the sink. A moist towel hung on the rack and fresh shaving cream sat in a container, next to a straight razor.

Marley blinked again and found himself in the bathroom, yes, but it was now dry and dark, the tiles cracked and filthy. No shaving cream or razor sat by the sink, no towel hung on the rack, no water dripped from the dry faucet.

Chapter 7

In the morning, Marley was awakened by the sound of a bird who'd made its nest on top of one of the paintings. A ray of sunshine flickered through a tear in one of the curtains. He stepped out the front door to relieve himself, enjoying the beautiful dawn, the sun just rising over the tall brick fence and lighting up the dilapidated porch. He stood quietly, listening to the morning birds as he ate the fruit and water he'd brought.

He decided he'd check out the kitchen again and, stepping in, was astonished to see that not only were all the pans in their proper place, all the knives were too, except for the one he'd taken and the missing one. He wondered if he'd dreamt about the rattling pans, the footsteps on the stairs, and the two ghosts in the bedroom.

Marley wrote in his ledger, "There was no trace of a living soul. There were, however, many traces of a spirit or a soul that could not be encountered or approached." After writing this entry, the reporter packed up the cedar box into his backpack along with his other supplies and rolled up his sleeping bag. Just as he stepped to the front door, he heard the distinct sound of laughter coming from upstairs. He decided not to follow it, instead, making his way through the front yard weeds. When he reached the iron gate it seemed to open on its own.

Over coffee at Mabel's later that day, Allie listened spellbound as Marley related all that had happened.

"See! I TOLD you it was haunted," she said.

"Indeed," he agreed. "We need to find out more about the brother, Bobby. We already discovered that he disappeared soon after returning from the war."

"Maybe he just got tired of arguing with his brother and headed back North to be with people whose philosophy he agreed with," Allie suggested.

Marley shrugged. "I suppose that's likely. Also he could have died from natural causes or an accident, medicine offered little aid in those days."

Allie looked around the café before leaning in to whisper, "You're thinking that Daniel killed his brother and buried him in that tomb, then boarded up the entry behind the fireplace, aren't you? I bet it's Bobby's ghost haunting the mansion."

Marley finished off his pie while he considered. "I suppose. But then, why did I see two ghosts? Why is there a servant hanging around? And what about the mysteries of the missing knives and disarrayed pans?"

He quieted as Mabel came up to refill their coffee cups.

"I gotta admit I was wrong about you, Mr. Robbins," she said.

"How so?"

"I never figured you to amount to anything. Those first few shows when all you were coming up with was local gossip, well, I guess that was sort of interesting too. But those reports you've been making about the old Greenwell mansion have got the town buzzing. You two thinking of buying the old place and fixin' it up? Could be made into a museum or something."

Marley and Allie stared at each other.

"Um... well, we hadn't actually thought about it."

"No?" Mabel snorted. "I could just see you two there, two fuddy-duddy nerds in an old dilapidated haunted house. Ha ha! Seems perfect to me!" She wandered away, chuckling to herself.

"Buy it?" Allie grasped her napkin in her hands. "Oh, Marley! Do you think we could? Wouldn't that be just heavenly? I mean, we'd have to get rid of the ghosts, first, but if we could, can you just imagine? That big old historic place all fixed up?"

"Just wait 'til you see it inside! It's incredible! Carved staircases, crystal chandeliers, and a humongous dining table. All the upholstery, drapes, and curtains are ruined by age, of course. What do you think it would take?"

"Let's find out!"

At the courthouse on Monday Marley was told that the city had taken possession of the property for unpaid taxes. The official there informed him that for $40,000 in back taxes he could own the property, including all the furnishings.

"Before we decide to buy it, I've got to see this for myself," Allie said. Marley agreed, and the next morning right after their tapings she drove them back to the mansion for Allie's first look inside.

Allie stood outside the front door hugging herself tightly.

"Come on," Marley said, trying to loosen the grip she had on herself. "The ghosts only come out at night."

"Well … if you're sure." She let him lead her into the house and one step in she stopped still, her jaw falling open. "Why … why … it's even more fantastic than I had dreamed! Look at that chandelier. All the antique furnishings. Oh, and the fireplace, wow, wow, wow!"

For four hours she walked all over the house, taking two hundred photos on her cell phone. She swooned at the huge displays of cooking and dining pieces.

"If we ever should get this house," she said, "I'd want to modernize the kitchen. You do know I'm a pretty good cook, huh?"

Marley grinned widely. "Don't forget you've been sharing your leftovers with yours truly for the past three weeks. Since only you and your Dad live in the house, I figured it likely that you were the cook. And, of course, you're always looking up recipes in magazines and online."

Together they went room by room, sketching out the floor plan, upstairs and down.

"How would we ever restore all this?" she asked. "It's going to take months and a bucket of money. How much cash do you have?"

"I'm barely making my school debt payments, rent, and food with the pittance I'm earning from Mr. Cohen," he admitted. "I guess once we buy it, I can live here and won't be paying rent." He flicked a spider off the arm of one of the chairs. "How about you?"

"I've got just over a thousand dollars in the bank. Maybe we can sell a few of the mansion's pieces and use that money for restoration," Allie suggested. "I know an antique dealer in Atlanta –

we could send him pictures of some of the pieces and see what he suggests."

"Yeah, maybe. But we can't do that until we come up with the $40,000 in advance. I don't see a bank loaning us that much money."

They looked at each other sadly until Allie's eyes brightened. "Say, didn't you say you'd found some old coins in the house? My dad collects coins. Maybe he'll loan us the money based on those coins and these pictures I've taken."

"Great! I've been wanting to meet your father and see where you live. Maybe I can get a home cooked meal out of this deal, too."

"Oh, you'll love my dad. Everyone does. Got a heart of gold."

Chapter 8

"So, you're the young man my Allison's been talking about?"

"Dad!"

Mr. Burton chuckled. Mostly balding, with only a monk's rim of hair over his ears and around the back, his jolly face glowed around his sparkling eyes and heavy jowls. Sitting behind his big desk, he reached forward to shake Marley's hand.

"I must say," he continued, "you're the first fellow Allison's showed the least interest in during her twenty-two years. I can see you're just as nerdy as she is."

"Dad!" she shouted again. "If you're going to be rude, we'll just leave."

He laughed out loud. "Okay, okay. Sorry Little Doe." He turned to Marley. "I call her Little Doe. Did she tell you that?"

Marley shook his head. "We're just friends, sir. In fact, we've only known each other for three weeks."

"Doesn't take long to fall in love, now does it?"

"I said we're just friends, sir."

He chuckled. "Yes, I heard you. So, what can I do for you, young fellow?"

Marley pulled the bag out of his pocket and handed it across the desk. "We were wondering if you'd take a look at these coins I have. I'm in need of some money and Allie said you might tell us what they're worth."

The older man glanced into the bag and both eyebrows arched. Pulling over a large lighted magnifying stand from the corner of his desk, he extracted one coin with padded forceps and examined both sides carefully. He turned to his computer and scrolled through some screens.

Turning to Marley he asked, "Where did you get these?"

"Well I ..."

Allie interrupted, "He inherited them from his grandfather. They've been in the family a long time. Are they valuable?"

Mr. Burton put the first coin down and pulled out another one, also looking it up on the computer after he'd identified it. He proceeded to pull out each one, studying them for a minute each before setting it down, building an array of two rows of ten.

"Young man, you have a small fortune here. This first one, a 1910-D ten-dollar Indian Eagle is worth about $4500. This second one, a 1907 twenty-dollar Saint Gaudens, should fetch upwards of $2500. Just based on these two coins and a general survey of the twenty, I'd say this bag might be worth upwards of $50,000."

For a full minute Marley was too stunned to speak. Finally, he squeaked out, "Sir. Could you take these as collateral and loan me $40,000? Then you could sell them for me."

Mr. Burton looked from Marley to Allie and then back again. "Yes, I suppose so. Why?"

Marley glanced at Allie who indicated that he should answer.

"Well, it's like this, sir," Marley said. "We, that is, Allie and I, we're thinking of buying a house together. You know, an investment."

Mr. Burton sat back in his chair, his hands grasped together in his lap. "Really, now. You two claim to just be friends and yet you're talking about putting a down payment on a home, huh? Well, young love can be impetuous I suppose. Where are you looking? That new subdivision north of town, what's it called, 'The Oaks'?"

"Actually, sir, the $40,000 is the total selling price. We're looking at the old Greenwell mansion. We can get it for past taxes."

Thumbing his fingers against the desk, Mr. Burton stared at his daughter. "The old Greenwell mansion huh? That place has been neglected for forty years. It must be a total wreck. Before you invest in such a place, you'd want to go inspect it from the inside …"

He paused and looked at the coins again. "From your grandfather, huh? Well, I guess I'd better not ask any more questions. Okay, you want to risk $40,000 and your reputation on an old fixer-upper … why not? I'll come with you now to the courthouse and see if we can sign the papers."

Chapter 9

Allie came out with the spaghetti and meatball dish she'd prepared, and everyone took a helping. After a prayer they dug in, Marley clearly relishing the home cooking. He had thirds.

"I used to be able to eat like that," Mr. Burton said with a sigh.

"And look where it got you." Allie pointed to her father's stomach. "Don't you even think about seconds."

"Don't be a young whippersnapper, Little Doe. Don't forget I just helped you buy a house."

Allie kissed his cheek. "Oh, yes. Thanks again, Dad. Really, I still can't believe it's ours! All that historic data and valuable antiques! It's an amazing buy."

"Yep, the whole kit and caboodle," Marley replied. He looked over at Mr. Burton who gave him a wink.

"Now you'll just have to figure out how you're going to be able to afford to restore and maintain it," Mr. Burton said. "Or maybe you'll just want to strip the insides and level the place."

Marley shook his head vigorously. "Oh no, Mr. Burton. We plan to fix it up and live there the rest of our lives."

After the dishes were put away, Allie loaded her cell phone photos onto her laptop and the three of them studied the pictures. They tried to price some of the items online, but the condition of the pieces made their job difficult.

"I think your idea of getting professional assessors involved is a good one," Mr. Burton noted.

He suggested they make a list of what needed to be done to make the place livable. On top of the list were the desperate repairs, like fixing all the broken windows, putting on a new roof, hiring an exterminator, and cleaning out all the ruined carpets and drapes. Then came the major installations, like plumbing, electricity, insulation, and gutters. Allie reminded him that she needed an updated kitchen, and he put that next. It seemed like furnishings would have to wait.

Mr. Burton wondered whether it would be worth seeing if the house could be made into a historic landmark. He helped them look up the procedures to apply for the designation, and then helped them locate corporations that would donate money to rebuild those types of places. Allie promised to fill out the grant applications.

The Atlanta antique dealer replied to Allie's email promptly and said he could come down Saturday, in two days. He arrived at nine, and spent several hours going through the items, though he had already made most of his decisions based on the photos Allie had sent him. The antique draperies, he reported, were ruined and should be scrapped. Most of the carpets had also been destroyed by the rodents. However, the furniture could be reupholstered, and several of the pieces were collector items, including various items in the kitchen and bedrooms, particularly some of the antique armoires and cedar chests. He gave Allie a list of twelve furniture items he thought might fetch the most money, ranging in value from two to fifteen thousand dollars. He also gave her a price list for reupholstering, which would be required before any of the chairs could be sold. By far, the most valuable pieces were the gold frames around the photographs. At the current price of gold, the fourteen frames would fetch between $3000 and $20,000 each, based on their weight. In addition, he recommended that the jewelry be appraised as individual pieces by a specialist he knew in Atlanta named Roger Striker. He suggested that when they were ready, they could bring the pieces up.

Marley and Allie were delighted! They chose two of the furniture pieces to sell and six of the frames, bringing in forty thousand dollars. With cash in the bank, they began the restoration in earnest.

Over the next two weeks, the two spent every spare hour cleaning their home. They took bids from electricians and plumbers and contracted out both of those jobs. Allie selected the new appliances to be installed in the kitchen and bathrooms, as well as the new fixtures and drapes to go throughout the house.

Every night at the television studio, Marley devoted fifteen minutes of his broadcast to the house and the progress he and Allie were making, using videos they created with the studio's equipment. On each segment, he discussed a bit about the mansion's history, how the repairs were progressing, and some of the pieces they'd discovered. Mr. Cohen was delighted with the enthusiasm the show had generated in town, bringing him advertisements from local dealers. He was able to give both Allie and Marley raises.

Chapter 10

One evening, sitting together at Allie's kitchen table, they opened the small cedar box Marley had brought back that first day. Inside, they found stacks of letters tied in ribbons. There were five bundles, each from a different correspondent.

The first stack was a set written from Sarah to Thomas. Allie and Marley giggled as they read the formalized communication, not the kind of love notes that normally would pass between happily married couples. On the one about Daniel's birth, for example, she had printed his tiny fingerprints on the bottom of the page, documenting his vital statistics of birth, weight, height, and time of birth. She said he was a fussy baby and commented on the slave nursemaid she was using for his breast feeding. There were no words of endearment in the letter, either to her husband or about her baby. The one about Bobby's birth, was different. Although it too had his fingerprints and birth facts, it had a more loving tone, describing him as a sweet and lovable child.

The next stack they went through was from a cousin from Virginia. Daniel and he had corresponded off and on over the years, and according to the letters, twice he'd visited, once in

1858 when George was twenty-one and on his honeymoon on a tour of the South, and then ten years later, when Daniel was in the midst of supporting the town of Greenwell. The last letter read as follows.

28 October, 1868.

Dear Daniel,

Let me express again my appreciation for the wonderful hosting you provided Kathleen and I this summer. Those evenings on the veranda with the mint julips will forever be in our memories. It's good to see that the old time South has not completely disappeared off the face of this once great nation.

I again apologize for my wife's persistence in asking about Bobby. She apologizes as well, and repeats she didn't mean to offend you and only asked because she had met him on our first visit.

She also tells me that she talked to one of your servants, a black girl named Olive. That nigger said that the old family servant, Joseph, disappeared the same weekend as did Bobby. Kathleen had been very impressed with Joseph and how devoted he was to your family. She wanted me to ask, if the question won't offend you, if you think they ran away together? You know how she is with the family tree, always trying to fill in the details.

Again, we offer great appreciation for your kind hosting and would be delighted to return the favor if you should ever find the time to come Virginia way.

Sincerely,

Your cousins, George and Kathleen Kirkpatrick

A few days later, during the refurbishing of the kitchen, the plumber asked Marley about access through the basement.

"Basement?"

The plumber explained, "The original pipes from the sink seem to dip into a space below the house, and I can feel a musty cold coming in around them, so I assume you gotta have a basement or at least a crawlspace. I don't know how to access it, though. Sometimes in these old houses there's a trapdoor in the pantry."

After the workmen had all left for the day, Marley went into the pantry that still held shelves of old mason jars. When he moved toward the back of the closet, he felt some of the floorboards shifting under his feet and, pulling them away, discovered a large metal hatch covering an opening to a cellar. He descended carefully, the old wooden ladder inside creaking with each step.

The musty cellar was about 20 by 40 feet with a dirt floor. Without a single window for ventilation, Marley's flashlight provided the only illumination. As he stepped around the room, he noticed that the ground was mostly firm underfoot, but softer in places. Each time he stepped on a soft area, he imagined he could hear a faint moan.

Along the walls, Marley discovered deteriorated nameplates hammered into the brick, one positioned at the end of each soft spot. One held the name Sarah, and he realized this must be Sarah Greenwell's grave, Thomas' wife. Most of the other plates were too rusted to read, but the last one shined in his light, seemingly untouched by age. In proud justified letters, he read "Joseph."

"He must have been very highly thought of, indeed, to be buried in the family tomb," he whispered.

Chapter 11

By the end of two months, the house had been stripped of all the moldy curtains and carpets, the hardwood floors polished, electricity wired, plumbing piped, a new roof shingled, air conditioning installed, and broken windows replaced.

One night after dinner at Allie's, Marley told her he was ready to move permanently into the house.

"Are you sure you want to spend the nights there with those ghosts?" Allie asked him, holding both his hands in a vise-like grip.

"I gotta," he said. "I can't keep paying rent and, well, the ghosts aren't going to hurt me after all."

"Okay, let me give you a kiss for luck." She bent forward and kissed him on the cheek, and Marley felt himself blush.

"You know, I really like you," he told her.

She laughed. "I could tell. I really like you, too! Maybe someday we'll do something more than have chaste kisses, you think?"

She drove him to the mansion's property, and he waved at her from that old iron gate, watching her wave back and then drive away. The sun had just set and the night owl had begun its hooting. Marley walked into the house and flipped

on the living room light, admiring how nice the
room looked, open and airy, with the two
refurbished chairs and table set up in front of the
fireplace. He turned off the light and climbed the
polished staircase to his room, the one which had
once been Thomas and Sarah Greenwell's so
many years ago. He'd retained all the old
furniture, the armoire, dresser, and bed frame,
adding a new mattress and a small end table with
a lamp and alarm clock. He showered and brushed
his teeth, and then tucked himself into the fresh
cotton sheets, smiling to himself at the success he
and Allie had made of refurbishing the home.

About midnight, Marley was awakened by
the sound of footsteps on the creaking floor in the
hallway. He grabbed his flashlight and listened at
his bedroom door. Looking down, he saw a
flickering light coming from the opening below
his door. He jumped into the hallway, and looking
down towards the far end, saw a lamp emitting a
hazy dismal type of light. It seemed to be dancing
from one bedroom doorway to another.

"Who's there?" Marley shouted.

No answer came, but the lamp seemed to
melt into the doorway at the end of the hall, the
room that used to be Bobby's. When he reached
it, he saw a faint light coming from beneath the
crack at the bottom of the door. From inside the
room he heard a faint singing, a melody like one

of the old slave songs. In moments both the singing and the light faded away. He opened the door and turned on the overhead light, finding the room empty, just as it had been when he last saw it.

He turned off the light and headed back to his own bed, snuggling into the still warm sheets. He wondered who could be the ghost and why was he haunting the mansion? He soon fell asleep, dreaming of ghosts and Civil War heroes.

At the studio the next morning, Allie was waiting eagerly for Marley to come in and tell how his night in the mansion had gone.

"Did you see any ghosts?" she demanded.

"Well, maybe." He told her about the sound of footsteps in the hallway, the flickering light that disappeared into Bobby's room, and the singing he'd heard. Just as he was finishing, a knock came at the studio's door

She gave him a mischievous smile. "I have a surprise for you."

He raised an eyebrow. "Yeah?"

She rushed over to the door and opened it to reveal a short thin man with a bushy black beard. He wore a black trench coat and a strange black hat covering unruly gray hair.

He followed her over to where Marley was standing and held out his hand.

"Marley, let me introduce you to Mr. Simone Gartham. Simone, this is Marley Robbins."

"Pleasure to meet you," the fellow said, shaking Marley's hand vigorously. "I've been following your reports about the Greenwell mansion, hoping we'd get a chance to talk."

Marley nodded. "You're into the occult, Mr. Gartham? A ghost hunter I would say."

The fellow stepped back, a surprised look to his eyes. "Call me Simone. Allie must have told you about me, huh?"

Marley shook his head. "No. I saw the occult pentagram necklace you're wearing, the EMF meter on your belt, and the ghostbuster tattoo on your left wrist."

Simone laughed. "Very observant, young man. Allie invited me to film for your show, talking with you about ghosts."

Allie helped set up the studio and cameras for the filming, and the two settled into chairs in front of the green screen. After the usual introduction material, including the local police report and weather, they had a talk about ghosts.

"The main thing I want to know," Marley said, "is why the house is being haunted. What makes a ghost?"

Simone stroked his beard, considering his answer carefully. "There can be different reasons, such as guarding a treasure, an unfinished mission, or searching for something valuable they lost, particularly a child. But by far the most common reason is that the person was murdered in the home and the murderer was never punished."

"You've mentioned different ways of getting rid of ghosts," Marley said, "like burning sage and using holy water. Would that work for ghosts looking for revenge?"

"No. When the ghost represents an unsolved murder victim, the only way to release them from their hauntings is to reveal the murderer, and then rebury the bodies with a proper funeral."

That afternoon, as Marley sat working at the old rolltop desk, he noticed an envelope crunched up in a cubbyhole. He squinted at it, pretty sure it hadn't been there before, but unsure if maybe he had just overlooked it. Pulling and straightening it out, he found that it was an old Western Union Telegraph, still sealed. Inside he found an original teletype, just like the kind that was used in the 1800s. There was no date on the sheet, merely the words "Please bring him to justice."

He wondered if maybe he'd brought it in with some other papers from the mail and had absent-mindedly stuck it in that slot. Looking up the number on the Internet, he called the local Western Union office and asked if they had delivered a telegram to his house over the past few days. They assured him that they had no record of the transaction and, furthermore, Western Union had discontinued delivering telegraph messages in 2006.

Chapter 12

The next weekend came their scheduled trip to Atlanta. Allie had made reservations for two rooms at the Holiday Inn and they each brought an overnight bag. Allie picked out three pieces of the jewelry from the house to bring to the appraiser and they got an early start. It was only a four-hour drive, and they talked non-stop the whole way. They shared so many interests, such as history, journalism, and the house, that the trip seemed to fly by.

Their first stop was at Roger Striker's shop, the jeweler who specialized in estate pieces. Allie handed him the three pieces in a velvet bag, and the jeweler took them out one at a time, examining each carefully.

"One of the ways to estimate the value of jewelry is by the type of mounting used for the piece," the jeweler explained. He showed the couple where to look with the magnifying glass to read the symbol designating the gold purity. The stamps mostly read 18k or 24k.

"As you can imagine, each piece's value is based not only on its precious metal content, but also on its artistic value and history. This one, for example," he picked up a green stoned ring, "this Early Georgian turquois ring with a solid gold intricate weaving would probably fetch about

$1500 at most auctions. This one, what I'd describe as a black topaz crowned heart betrothal ring with foil wrappings and diamond chips, probably dates from about 1800. I'd estimate its value at about $1300. As you might have guessed, by far the most valuable is this Tahitian cultured pearl and diamond necklace strung on white gold. The alternating color scheme of these pearls is mesmerizing. I guess this one would top $30,000 in the right market."

"What would you give us for them?" Allie asked.

The jeweler stroked his chin, looking at the jewelry, then at Allie, and then back at the jewelry. "Well, I can give you 50% of my valuation for the two rings. That'd be $1400. The necklace is a bit beyond my operating expenses at the moment. I'll be happy to hold it and try to sell it for you for a 40% commission. Would you like to do that?"

Allie nodded. "Yes, that would be great!"

"Fourteen hundred dollars in cash! We're rich!" Marley exclaimed. He grabbed Allie and gave her a long, deep kiss. He had never done this before, but she didn't seem to mind so he kept on kissing.

Roger waited until they were done and cleared his throat.

Looking over at him, Allie said, "Oh, you look worried. What's wrong?"

Roger bit his lip. "I don't mean to pry into your personal business, but selling your antique jewelry might be something you regret later. You'll never be able to replace these pieces."

Allie gave a light laugh. "We still have plenty more at home."

"And when you've sold them all, then what?"

Allie and Marley looked at each other. "Well, I guess we'll have to figure out some other way to make money," she said.

Walking out with her purse and his wallet both bulging with cash, worries about the future quickly fluttered away. They picked one of the fanciest restaurants in town and enjoyed a scrumptious meal before heading to their hotel. The check-in line was long and it took almost forty-minutes before they got their turn at the front desk.

"Reservation under Allie Burton," she told the desk clerk.

He looked up her reservation and copied her license and credit card information. Handing her a card key, the clerk said, "Room 312. Good thing you got here before ten, otherwise we'd have released your room. It's the last one we've got."

Allie looked at the key, then up at the clerk, then back at Marley, and then back to the clerk. "There's only one key? I distinctly made reservations for two rooms."

The clerk checked the computer again. "Nope. Says here one room for two people. Sorry about that. You know this weekend both the Falcons and the Braves are playing, don't you? I doubt if you'll find another available room for a forty-mile radius."

Allie told Marley the news and the two of them went up to the room to look it over. It was a typical small hotel room, a single king bed with hardly a foot of space on either side. A small desk and chair hugged the wall next to a dresser that had a flat screen TV against the wall.

"I could sleep in the car?" Marley offered.

"Don't be silly. This bed's plenty big enough for the both of us."

He smiled shyly. "Well, if you don't mind, okay I guess. You know I'm a gentleman."

"Sometimes too much!" she said, stomping her foot.

He looked at her a bit confused, until she took his head in both hands, drawing it down to kiss him fully on the mouth. He kissed her back, and soon they found that a bed half that size still would have been big enough for them both.

Chapter 13

The next morning over breakfast, Marley held her hand as they ate.

"You know, the house is really big."

She sipped her coffee, looking at him from under her bangs. "Yes, that's true."

"Lots of bedrooms."

"Uh-huh."

He sighed, finishing off his scrambled eggs and starting on his toast. He threw it back onto the plate. "Look, what I'm trying to say is that maybe you should think about moving into the mansion, too. You know, to save rent and maybe so I'm not alone at night."

Allie picked up his hand and kissed it. "Hush, you silly shy man. Of course, I'd love to live with you. As soon as we get back, I'll pack up my stuff and, no, I won't need my own bedroom. I think we proved last night that one bed is sufficient for the two of us. There is one condition, though. You have to promise to protect me from the ghosts."

Marley gave her a big kiss. "You bet! They only come out at night and I'll be there by your side!"

They continued talking about their Atlanta adventure as they sipped their after-breakfast coffee.

"You know, we have a lot of very valuable items in the house. Once we get back, we should purchase a safe to store the more valuable keepsakes."

They did just that, and placed in all the house jewelry, securely locking it up. The next day Allie asked him to open it again to place her mother's wedding ring that she'd brought from home. When he opened it, the two were startled to find a telegram from Western Union sitting inside on top of the jewelry. Just like the first one there was a one-line teletyped message. This time it read, "My bones protect."

"What do you think it means?" Allie asked.

"Clearly there's something to do with bones. Maybe the ones in the family crypt in the cellar?"

"You said you think one of the ghosts might be that of the servant Joseph," Allie said. "Is that because both Bobby and he disappeared from the house at about the same time?"

"Yes, there's that. And one of the ghosts I saw seemed to be African American. But I was thinking about another strange thing. The first time I came into the house everything was covered in layers of dust – everything, that is, except for the pots and knives in the kitchen and the handrails on the staircase. I'm wondering if

Joseph, as family servant, didn't continue to take care of those things even after death."

Allie squinted at him. "That's pretty far-fetched."

"Hey, you're the one who believed in ghosts first! Anyway, yeah, I think Joseph is one of the ghosts. If this message refers to him, I guess we should go see what's in his crypt."

"Really? You want to go graverobbing?" Allie asked, her eyes large.

Marley shrugged. "I guess that's pretty gruesome, huh? You don't want to have any part of it?"

"Are you kidding? I can hardly wait. This is a part of archeology I never got to try. Let's borrow lights from the studio so we can light up that cellar. Drop a couple of shovels and bring a more reliable ladder, okay? Oh, and we'll need gloves and masks."

It took them a couple of hours to get it all set up. Marley fixed the twenty-foot aluminum ladder so that it made a secure access to the basement and lowered the two shovels. He dropped down an extension cord and, once on the ground inside, set up three bright lights they'd borrowed from the studio.

They found Joseph's grave at the corner of the room and the two of them began digging. It took half an hour to scrape out the dirt and reveal the wooden coffin, the top of which gave way to a sharp blow from Marley's shovel. They pulled out the wooden pieces and found a set of desiccated human bones. Focusing their lights inside the coffin, they saw something shiny in the middle of the skeleton's chest. Allie reached down into the coffin and pulled out the object. They both gasped, recognizing its identity immediately. It was the missing kitchen knife.

"Do you think…?"

Allie cocked her head at Marley. "What?"

"Well," he continued, "I'm just wondering if one could get fingerprints off a knife that's been buried for a hundred and fifty years. Do you remember what that ghost hunter said? Gartham was his name wasn't it? He said if the murderer could be revealed and the body reburied, that would put the ghost to rest."

"Hey, it's worth a try!"

Allie placed the knife carefully in a plastic bag and the next morning contacted Detective Drake, the city's police detective. He followed them down to inspect the graves and then sat at the kitchen table with them, examining the knife.

"Families sometimes buried their loved ones in cellars in those days," Drake explained. "It was to protect them from grave robbers. I could ask the state forensics to get involved if you want. As far as fingerprints, though, our records only go back fifty years. You'd have to have a set of the fingerprints of the suspected killer so we'd have something to compare these with."

Allie's eyes lit up. "We DO have a set of his fingerprints … well, a set of fingerprints from the person we suspect did the murders." She turned to Marley. "Go get the stack of letters from Sarah we went through."

He smiled. "Right. One of them had a set of Daniel's fingerprints as an infant." He asked the detective if that would do and Drake said it would.

When Marley got back with the letter, he said there might be a second murder too. He didn't want to go into details yet, but if they found another weapon, could they call him back? With assurances that they could, Detective Drake left with the knife and a photograph of the fingerprinted letter.

"You're thinking those are Bobby's bones behind the fireplace, aren't you?" Allie asked.

"Yep! You up for another round of gravedigging?"

She gave him a huge grin. "You bet! Let's go for it."

Removing the grate, Marley crawled into the back of the fireplace carrying a hammer and chisel. He'd had one of the repairmen plaster the inside, so it took him nearly an hour to break that out and remove the bricks wide enough to again gain entry to the tomb. He crawled through the hole first, and then took in and set up the light that she fed him through the hole. Its stark slate luminescence created a ghostly shimmer in the room. He then helped Allie wiggle in.

She looked around, astounded. "Wow! I mean, we've discovered lots of little hiding places all over this house. Remember the one in the upstairs sitting room that held all those old bottles of liquor behind the portrait? But, really, how did we miss this huge place when we sketched out the floor plans?"

Marley gave her a thumbs up. "One of the many great advantages of having a creepy old mansion to explore. After we move Bobby's bones out, I think this place would be a great wine cellar."

She stepped over and kissed him, something they'd been doing a lot of since their Atlanta trip. "As usual, you're so right!"

Putting on their gloves, they lifted the lid off the sarcophagus and lowered it to the floor. On top, the sword glimmered in the reflected light. Lifting it carefully, they discovered that the hilt had a set of easily distinguishable bloody fingerprints, preserved against deterioration in the tomb. In addition, the blade had a dark crimson stain, clearly blood.

"So, Daniel used this sword to kill his brother, and then buried it with him in the fireplace. Wow."

Allie picked up the skull. "Look here. There's a big crack across the skull. It looks like it was smashed with something."

Marley's eyes widened. "Oh! Remember me telling you about my first night in the house? I found a large pan on the kitchen floor with a big round dent in the middle. I get it now. The ghosts were telling me that's how Daniel killed Bobby. He smashed in his head with the pan, and then stabbed him with his sword. Joseph must have tried to stop him, so Daniel grabbed a kitchen knife and killed him too!"

"Poor Bobby."

"And, hey, look at Bobby's forearm bones. They're sliced through. That's why the cleaver was missing that first night I stayed here. Daniel must have chopped through Bobby's arm to get the sword. Hmm. I can picture the whole fight in my mind."

Allie shivered. "No wonder the house is haunted! Well, once we turn this sword over to Detective Drake we'll have proof that Daniel killed these two. We can arrange for their proper burial and then the ghosts won't come back." She noticed that Marley's attention was focused on the inside of the coffin. "Something else wrong?"

Reaching around the body and under the bottom of the muslin shroud, Marley scooped out a piece of glittering metal. Showing it to Allie she let out a loud whistle. "A gold bar! Look, it has the stamp of the Confederacy!"

Carefully moving Bobby's bones aside, they lifted the edge of the muslin to reveal that the bottom of the tomb was lined with what seemed like scores, maybe even a couple of hundred similar gold bars.

"Daniel must have brought these back from the war and buried them here. Marley, oh Marley, we're rich beyond our wildest dreams!"

Chapter 14

Over supper that evening, the two toasted
their new found wealth with a delicious wine
Allie had bought, along with the roast chicken she
prepared. They feasted, talking about how
wonderfully happy they were.

"You know," Allie said, "there're still a lot
of mysteries we haven't solved about this house."

"Oh? How's that?"

"Well, for one thing, we still don't know
why Nathan was such a hermit. Why are there no
pictures of him anywhere? Why is it he made sure
no one ever saw him his entire life? Do you
suppose he was incredibly deformed or
something?"

Marley chuckled. "You haven't figured that
out yet, huh? Seems pretty obvious to me."

Allie waited for a minute, but as he
continued to sit back looking smug, she picked up
a fork full of mashed potatoes and flung it at him.
He swatted it away just in time.

"Tell me!"

He chuckled. "So, we know that Daniel
never married, and that he liked to dabble with the
servants. It seems obvious to me that Nathan was
the result of one of his dalliances with a negress.
He decided to adopt the child and make him his
heir, but he didn't want the town seeing that he

had a half black child. He sent the boy off to Europe, and Nathan was perfectly happy to spend the rest of his life there, away from his mean father and the bigoted attitudes in Greenwell. When he had to come back, he chose to never let it be known he was a mulatto by never letting anyone but his servant see him. The servant was able to keep the secret, and so it died with Nathan's death."

"You are so clever, Marley. That's one of the reasons I love you so much." She kissed him again. "Anything else you haven't told me about Nathan?"

"Yep. Remember those strange objects on the shelf over his bed?"

"You mean the Ouija board and all that?"

"Exactly. Those are ways of communicating with ghosts. He had a bag with runes, too. Clearly, he was aware of the hauntings. I guess we'll never know if he actually communicated with them."

"Ooh," Allie whistled. "I bet we have even more mysteries to uncover."

After dinner, Allie and Marley were doing the dishes when Allie heard a strange moaning coming from the cellar.

"Do you hear that?" she asked.

"What?"

"Something coming from the cellar. Listen. Don't you hear it?"

Marley stood listening, and then shook his head. "I don't hear anything."

"Well I do, and I'm going to investigate."

Taking a flashlight, she climbed down the ladder that Marley had left in place and, reaching the ground, realized that the eerie moan came from one of the graves. As she stood immediately over the located grave, the ground began to slowly sink. She stepped onto a firm part of the floor, watching as the grave sank about 12 inches. With each inch the moaning grew louder.

"Oh, spirit from the past," Allie called, "Do you have a message for me?"

The walls of the dark room shook. Pointing her flashlight beam directly toward the grave, she saw a sparkle reflected in her light. She knelt and picked up a magnificently beautiful two-karat diamond solitaire ring. When she slipped it onto her finger the eerie sounds ceased, and all was calm.

"Hey, everything all right down there?" Marley called from the hatch in the pantry.

She climbed back up and, taking off the ring, dropped it in his palm. As soon as it left her finger the moaning from the basement resumed.

"Clearly the spirits want me to wear this," she said, reaching for it.

But Marley held it back. Going down on one knee he said, "Allison Burton, will you do me the great honor of becoming my wife?"

Allie grabbed her love and planted a big loving kiss on his eager lips. "YES, YES, YES."

She held out her hand and he slipped the ring on, and the moaning from below stopped.

Epilogue

Detective Drake confirmed that the fingerprints on the knife and sword were Daniel's. Marley's television shows explaining how Daniel had murdered his brother and servant were such great hits, they were picked up by national television. He got a job in Montgomery at a major affiliate as an investigative reporter.

Daniel's statue was taken down from the Town Green and replaced with an obelisk commemorating the slaves who died unheralded before 1860. All the graves in the cellar were inspected by the local and state authorities and an anthropologist from the State University said that the youngest grave was at least 150 years old. The bones of the deceased were dug up, including Bobby's from the tomb, and all reinterred in the local cemetery with proper ceremonies. Never again did a ghost haunt Greenwell mansion.

The gold bullion was sold, bringing in just over eighteen million dollars that Allie's father helped them invest properly, guaranteeing them to never have money worries again. Once the mansion and grounds were properly restored, Allie led visitors on tours, Wednesday afternoons from 2 to 4, describing the many historic items, photos, and period pieces, and the history of the house and area.

In June the two had a fabulous wedding, attended by everyone in town. And they lived happily ever after.

The Mysterious Mansion

Part 2

by Hank Roberts

Book Two:
The Mysterious
Mansion
Part II

PROLOGUE

This book is preceded by "The Mysterious Mansion". It is a continuation of that original story.

Marley and Allison Robbins, two energetic historians and investigative reporters, continue their lives living in an old mansion that they have refurbished. Many mysteries about the mansion have already been found, however the duo know that there are more to be discovered. Allison discovers, one evening, that one of the bedrooms in the mansion contains a locked and sealed closet, that no one has ever bothered to investigate. She knew that Nathan Greenwell lived in this bedroom and she knew that he was a man of many mysteries. What had he been working on for many years that caused him to be a recluse? How could his secrets about this home be disclosed? And, is there any such thing as time travel?

CHAPTER 1

Allison and Marley Robbins lived very comfortably in their refurbished mansion. They both were extremely interested in historical facts and they enjoyed living in an old historic plantation house. The residents of their small town had accepted the fact that the old Greenwell mansion was not actually haunted. It did have its share of mysteries, but the townsfolk were ready to accept the Robbins, their weird lifestyle, and the old mansion.

Because of the gold found under Bobby Greenwell's grave, the Robbins had no worries about finances or maintaining a comfortable lifestyle. Marley did enjoy going, periodically, to Montgomery and appear on the TV station there. He kept his job as investigative reporter, but he would not accept a salary. His main intention was to stay in the view of the public so he might promote any further historical discoveries that he or Allie might make.

Both Allie and Marley enjoyed making presentations to college and social groups. They were offered payment for their appearances, however they would give it back to the institution hosting the presentation, to be used for scholarships for history majors. History, archaeology, anthropology, they were all the same to this couple. They enjoyed promoting the education of those who chose to study these subjects. The Robbins would encourage the winners of the scholarships they set up and encouraged them to be open minded. They promoted the idea that

"Anything could be there, if only one would look hard enough."

Marley and Allison enjoyed spending time in Tuscaloosa, at the University of Alabama, where there was a large library chock full of history books, especially about the South. The library was a wonderland for any historical investigative reporter, especially these two. Because of their notoriety, they were afforded access to the entire library, along with its many research capabilities. Marley and Allie would often praise the well-equipped library and its extremely helpful staff.

On one visit to the library, Allie discovered an article that told of Nathan Greenwell, Daniel's son. It was noted that Nathan had very dark skin and prominent Negro features. This boy could not be accepted as a son of Daniel and a slave so at the age of two he was sent off to England where he lived in a boarding school. Daniel had sufficient money to afford to keep Nathan in England, at least as long as Daniel lived. Daniel would, however, visit Nathan each spring and bring him gifts and news of life on the Greenwell plantation.

Nathan received a very intensive education. He was fluent in several languages and was proficient in math and physics. After graduating from college, Nathan worked for a short time in England as a mechanical and physical engineer.

When Daniel died, Nathan was 23. He decided to return to the old Greenwell plantation, where he was born, even though he believed due to his skin color he would not be welcomed by the local residents. He vowed to live the life of a recluse within the mansion.

CHAPTER 2

Since Tuscaloosa was only an hour drive from their home, Allison would often find herself visiting the library several times a week. She had something specific that she was very interested in researching. Here at the University was an ideal location with its wealth of stored knowledge about many topics for Allie to delve as deep as she pleased into any particular subject.

Her mind couldn't help but wander to thoughts about the strange objects that she and Marley had found on the shelf above Nathan's bed. What was the purpose of the Ouija board? What was it there for and who used it? And there was no apparent reason for the bag that contained 24 different tiles, each containing one strange letter. There must have been some logical reason for the presence of these items. But what?

As Allison conducted her in depth research into the objects that were found in Nathan's room, she was cautious not to arouse the interest or suspicion of any of the workers in the library. They already thought that she was a little touched, but Allie didn't want any further inquiries.

"Ok," said Allison to herself. "All I have to do is research a few simple objects. A Ouija board, a set of runes, a crystal ball, a metallic spherical ball, and a voodoo doll. What could be easier than that?"

When the runes were researched, it was found that they were a set of 24 stones. On each of these stones was inscribed a single letter. These letters were used to create words before the Greek alphabet was accepted for common use. Allie could not determine any possible use for these stones by Nathan Greenwell. He could read and write in English, French, and Latin. Why would he want to rely on an archaic set of outdated letters? She knew that the voodoo doll was often used to place spells and hexes on other unsuspecting persons. The crystal ball was often used by those who claimed to be able to see into the future. No substantial evidence could be located to prove that it was anything more than a crystal sphere.

The Ouija board was found to be a spiritual type medium, through which the user could gain answers to questions that were otherwise unanswerable. This type of device, related to witchcraft and sorcery, was most often used by people of a dark spiritual nature.

The metallic spherical structure required more extensive research. When Allie approached the librarians with the subject of a metallic sphere, she was guided to hundreds of various locations to research. Her research led her to topics of perpetual motion, space travel, time travel, energy production and many others. As she read through the many references, she continued to think back on how any of these uses would be used by or effect the life of Nathan Greenwell.

She realized that Nathan would have been exposed to stories about time travel and even perpetual motion. Many scientists of his day had been experimenting with these subjects. None of them had devised a reasonable means by which their ideas could be proven, of course. Many of the inventors and scientist also delved into alchemy, again without success. There were so very many things that stimulated the curiosity of the people of the early 1900s, very few of which were ever proven.

Marley was always excited to meet with Allie when she got home from Tuscaloosa. They would spend hours talking about the different finds that she had made during her research.

On one particular evening, Allison returned with some provocative news. She had found that it was believed, during the early 20th Century, that metallic spheres were related to, and used in, the development of time travel. Often the early researchers would put people in large spherical metal containers in an attempt to send them into another time dimension. This transformation could never be proven, but it was tested on more than one occasion by the scientists of that day. She also found that the letters inscribed in the 24 runes were supposed to be able to communicate with beings from ancient times, when encountered by any of the space travelers.

When this information was shared with Marley, both historians agreed on the fact that Nathan must have been researching some type of time travel. At least now they could pinpoint the direction in which their own research must proceed. Was there anything that they had overlooked, within the massive mansion?

The Robbins had found all of Nathan's possessions, which were very few. There was a rag doll, a spherical metal ball, a set of 24 tiles with some type of letter inscribed into them, and a Ouija board. There were some old clothes and slippers, all of which didn't amount to much.

CHAPTER 3

After long contemplations about everything that had been heard and found in their new home, Marley remembered that they had not bothered to remove the locks or investigate the small closet which was located in Nathan's bedroom. The closet was very small and didn't seem to be of any significance, however, with all of the other weird findings there was no telling what would be found within that closet. Certainly, it was worth taking a look.

With hammer, chisel, saw, and wire clippers in hand, the two curious investigators proceeded to Nathan's bedroom where they planned to open the door to the small closet. This closet was secured with several locks and some metal straps, which were bolted to the door and wall. Marley spent several hours sawing on the hard metal locks before finally cutting them off. The metal the locks were composed of seemed so strange, he decided to submit them for analysis to the science department at the University.

It took the couple a complete day to fully remove all the objects which secured this door. When they finally could look into the closet, all they could see was a small empty room. The dimensions were 3' X 5'. There were no clothes hangers nor any movable structures. There was only a dusty old room with wooden slats for the walls and floor. Nothing appeared to be odd or different about this small space. What could it have been used for and why was it so securely closed? This appeared to be another dimension of this mysterious mansion.

One-night Allison found it impossible to sleep. She woke Marley and told him of her recurring thoughts about the secret closet. "I must satisfy my curiosity about this mystery before it drives me insane," she told her husband. "I'm going to get up and see if I can find any more answers to our dilemma."

She slipped on some jeans and a floppy old denim shirt. Her slippers, which she put on, were right at the side of her bed. Allie left their bedroom and proceeded to the bedroom which had been occupied by Nathan.

When she turned on the light in Nathan's room, she heard a distinct swish of air that was coming from the small closet. She proceeded to the closet and opened the door, which had previously been locked tight. As she stood and observed the small space, she noticed a loose board on the floor, from which came the sound of escaping air. When she touched the board it moved slightly, allowing a dim beam of light to pass through.

"Where could that light be coming from?" Allie wondered.

Squatting down beside the loose board, Allison tried, in vain, to move it. It was securely attached but it was slightly loose. Her curiosity began to run away with her as she thought of the different ways that she might get the board to move and provide her with a view of what was beneath. The tension in her mind and body now grew to a great crescendo of excitement.

Allison stepped back to the shelf in the room where Nathan's objects of curiosity remained. In one hand she lifted the metal sphere and in the other she secured the odd-looking voodoo doll. Not knowing why, she chose these two items, she cautiously stepped back to the small closet.

It was hard for her to decide whether she should call for her husband to accompany her in this adventure. Marley would probably not be interested, unless she uncovered something that was really a showstopper. He had been exposed on many occasions to the mundane discoveries that they had made. Now it would take something really shocking to get his attention.

Alone and slightly trembling, Allie proceeded to the small dark closet. She placed the small voodoo doll in her shirt pocket. The head of the doll stuck out, as though the doll was watching her every move. With the metal sphere secure in both hands, Allison proceeded to a position which brought her directly over the loose board in the floor. Twisting and turning the metal structure, Allie tried to induce some type of response. Nothing happened.

She then stepped back out of the dark closet and into the light of the bedroom. There she turned the sphere in all types of positions, trying to see if there were any markings on it. After about two minutes of close scrutiny, Allie discovered an extremely small "N" stamped into one position on the ball. "I wonder what this N stands for?" she asked herself. "Did Nathan stamp it here to indicate that this was his possession? Was it stamped here to indicate what type metal was used in its construction? Perhaps it indicated the direction north."

Allison oriented herself in the room to determine the true position of north. She positioned her finger over the N on the ball and then reentered the closet. Standing directly over the loose board, she pointed the N toward magnetic north and held the sphere very still. The ball began getting warmer and warmer until it was difficult to hold. The closet floor trembled and a 2½' X 3' opening appeared, directly under her. There was a stairway that led down from the newly made opening in the floor. "Now where could this possibly lead?" she pondered.

Being the inquisitive investigator that she was, she cautiously began descending the stairs. When she reached the floor of the room beneath, faint voices could be heard coming from the adjacent room. Allison still had her bedroom slippers on so she could move silently across the floor and peek into the next room.

She observed that the adjoining room was a large dining room. There was a very large dining table where the entire Greenwell family sat dining. A stately, proper man, whom she suspected was Tom Greenwell, sat in the massive chair at the end of the table. Allison could hear him barking out orders to his family members.

"Those 10 acres up by the house require cultivating and planting immediately, if we plan to have any decent truck patch for our meals and canning. The darkies already got their acre planted and its coming along fine. You boys take some of those pickneys with you and get that planting done."

Allison noticed a teenage servant moving away from the table and headed in her direction. She jerked back out of sight, knocking the voodoo doll out of her shirt pocket. It fell directly in the middle of the hallway. As the servant reached that area, she bent down and picked up the doll. "My dol," she exclaimed. "How in de worl dis cums to bees heae? Dis dol be missin fer bout a year now." The girl took the doll and proceeded around the corner where she ran directly into Allie.

"Ghoost," she tried to scream out. She was too frightened to say much of anything. Blood had rushed from her face and she had turned almost completely white. Allison hurried toward the girl and placed her hand over her mouth. "I'm not a ghost but a friendly visitor," Allie told the girl. "You must not tell anyone of our meeting, or I will come back and haunt you." The negro girl, trembling and dazed, squatted down beside the small table located there. "No mizz, I won tell no one lest they fetch me and beat me sometin terribl'."

As quickly and quietly as possible, Allison stepped back to the stairway, from which she had come. When reaching the top, she secured the metal sphere and turned the N toward true north. A trembling feeling once again encompassed the floor and the access to the lower level closed. She found herself, again, standing in the dark closet.

As Allie stood in the bedroom awe stricken, she contemplated what had just happened. This was an earth-shaking finding, but should she go directly and wake Marley and tell him? Perhaps not. Not until morning when they could both properly investigate this new mystery of their special mansion. She slipped quietly back into her and Marley's bedroom, removed her slippers, and snuggled back into bed, pulling up the covers.

"Boy do I have some news to share with my hubby when we wake up tomorrow," Allie whispered to herself as she drifted off to sleep.

CHAPTER 4

Allie and Marley woke up as the first ray of sunshine made its way through the pulled curtains in their bedroom. Marley saw the "mule eating briars" look on Allie's face. Before she could speak, he turned to her and said, "Whatever crazy discovery you have made will surely wait until we can get some breakfast."

They did their usual morning activities and dressed in comfortable clothes. Marley went outside to grab the daily newspaper and Allison went to the kitchen and began cooking eggs, bacon and "store bought" biscuits. She always wanted to make the biscuits that were made from scratch, but she never seemed to find the time.

Settled at the breakfast table and enjoying their first cup of coffee, Marley turned to his wife and said, "OK. I'm ready. Let's hear whatever great discovery you've made." Allie began babbling away with all of the details about the time warp closet.

"Slow down, slow down," Marley shouted. "I can hardly understand a word that you are saying. Start again from the point where you went to Nathan's bedroom last night."

Allie composed herself and explained in great detail all that she had experienced the preceding evening, including her brief visit to the 19th century.

After finishing her descriptions of the previous night's activities and pouring them both another cup of coffee,

Allison gazed across the table to see what Marley had to say.

"I knew that there was more to Nathan's being a hermit than met the eye. He not only wanted to remain unseen, he wanted to keep his private research work a secret." Marley finished his coffee. "Sounds like we're ready for a new adventure!"

Before they would endeavor to make a journey to the Greenwell mansion of the 1800s, they agreed that they would like to take some gifts. They decided they had to remember that they would not be able to take something which would change the course of history. History, from the 1800s to the 2000s had already been established. People had lived their lives and situations had occurred that could not be changed.

Marley decided to secure a small amount of several different seeds for planting. He realized that agriculture had enjoyed many advancements and improvements since 1800. He researched the different types of crops that were being grown back in antebellum times and, using this information, he decided to collect some seeds of plants that weren't already being grown there. Marley collected a half pound small bag of different types of hybrid corn, some of which would grow much faster and produce higher yields than the corn that the Greenwells were currently growing. He also collected seeds for melons, squash, beans, beats, turnips and other vegetables that were regulars in the growing of a family garden. He figured these could help the Greenwells without changing the path of history. He placed the seeds in individual plastic bags and secured them in the back pouch of a jacket that he planned to wear on their journey.

Allison was just as picky about choosing something that she could take that would not affect future historical events. She would have liked to have been able to inform Bobby about the fact that his brother was going to kill him, but that would have altered history. She would also have liked to warn them of the impending war between the states, which was soon coming and would affect the lives of all Americans. Allie had to move away from these thoughts and think of something that she could take that would be valued in their time of history.

Finally, she decided to work toward taking something that would be used and appreciated by the ladyfolk of that time period. She knew that they could already sew and they knew how to make their own clothes. Cooking and canning were skills used by these people for future meals and for their simple necessities of living. What they didn't possess was different cosmetics, especially perfumes. When a girl married during that time, the only thing that was used to create a pleasant smell for the ladies was for her to carry a bunch of freshly picked flowers. Often friends would fix for the bride a small bundle of fresh flowers that she could wear under her outer clothing to improve the under washed body aroma.

Allison picked out items that were made in Paris and other European cities, where she was sure the Greenwells had no contact. She also included a few lipsticks, rouges, and scented body powders.

Allie's gift items were packed into a small canvas duffle bag, which she could easily throw over her shoulder. Inside of this small bag, she also packed a couple of changes of clothes. She didn't include particularly fancy outfits, since she realized that many of the ladies of the 1800s only owned one fancy dress and maybe two sets of work clothes. The couple wanted to fit into the pattern of life of the people who lived where they were going.

On the morning of their departure, the couple dressed in some work clothes, which were comprised of denim from top to bottom, low top used tennis shoes, and beat up baseball caps from different teams. Filled with excitement and wonder, they headed to Nathan's bedroom to try and reproduce Allie's adventure.

Marley secured the sphere and examined it, locating the N that Allie had told him about. The two explorers entered the small closet with Allison holding her finger over the N embossed on the metal sphere, just as she had done the night before, so that she would know the direction of magnetic north.

As the couple stood directly over the loose board on the floor of the closet, Allie removed her finger from covering the N. Again, the floor trembled and an entrance way was exposed beneath their feet. As Allie had reported to Marley, there was a stairway leading down to the room below.

When they reached the bottom of the stairs, they could hear voices of several children playing. When they peered into the adjacent room, they saw several white children dressed in makeshift grey military uniforms playing with make believe swords. The black children were sitting in a crowded group, over in the corner, watching the others play.

Marley and Allison decided that it would be best if they were to leave the house through the back door and come around to the front to make a formal entrance. They both knew the layout of the entire house for it was the house in which they were currently living. The only real change was the difference in time. They found themselves firmly transfixed into the 1800s. Neither of them knew how they would be received by the Greenwell family when they approached the front door and introduced themselves. Allie said, "You know the saying, nothing ventured nothing gained."

When the Robbins reached the front of the house, they found Tom Greenwell and two of his cousins sitting in three large rocking chairs on the front veranda.

"Let me do the talking," Marley whispered to Allison. "In these days the men usually did all the talking." Allie glanced back at him with a sarcastic expression on her face.

"Morning gentlemen. Are you the men of the house?" Marley blurted out. "My wife and I are investigative reporters and we would like to write an article about life on this plantation. If you would afford us this great pleasure, we will be happy to include you in any articles about the mansion that might be published."

The men seemed quite shocked at what seemed to them as very odd visitors. One of them spilled his iced tea onto the floor as he jumped back from the intrusive visitors. Mr. Tom Greenwell was a gentleman who was always desirous of special attention and this notoriety was something that pleased him very much. He invited the couple to come up onto the porch and enjoy some fresh sweet tea with him and his cousins.

There were eight large Corinthian columns supporting the huge porch, the first floor of the mansion, and the roof of the second floor. Leading up to the porch were twelve wide wooden steps, lined with huge decorative wooden banisters. The house, the banisters and the railings were all stark white, trimmed in bright green. The floor of the porch was a light grey, which helped disguise the many scuff marks from heavy work boots.

Once the Robbins were seated in their smaller rockers on the porch, they could easily view the massiveness of the great plantation. One of the black servants was called upon to bring two more glasses of tea. The group sat on the veranda for at least an hour engaging in small talk about the nearby farmers, the number of darkies that were present, the soon to be planted crops, and the weather. Tom inquired as to where Marley and Allie were staying and when he received the answer that they weren't exactly sure, he demanded that they stay there at the "big house." Marley immediately accepted and stated that this would give them even more time to interview Tom and his family.

From their viewpoint, there on the porch, Marley and Allie could clearly see a gravel road that led up to the house. On both sides of this road there were massive fields being worked by the slaves. There were 8 to 10 mules in each of the fields and at least 30 black workers plowing and planting. Each mule was hitched to, and drawing, a single plow which was driven by a black man. Black women followed behind the plows, each carrying and planting the different crop that was to be planted in that field. The smaller field to the right, as they were told by Tom, was being cultivated for growing vegetables, along with watermelons. There were about 165 acres on this side of the road. They were being planted with corn, different beans, collard greens, cucumbers, squash, turnips (along with their turnip greens), and other common crops.

The field on the left side was reserved for cotton. There was a total of 1,200 acres which were planted with this extremely profitable commodity. Behind the house was a smaller garden of only five acres, known as the family's truck patch, which contained watermelons and cantaloupes to be consumed by the family. There was a variety of fruit trees located all over the plantation. There was even 10 acres of pecan trees, which yielded a plethora of delicious nuts in the fall of each year.

CHAPTER 5

Tom Greenwell called out to one of his maid servants, "Mattie…get yourself in the back and kill some chickens. We need to fry up some special meal for our guests. Make some chitlin, corn bread, collards, and sweet taters – and make up a new batch of that sweet tea. I see Daniel and Bobby comin' up the road. They been supervising the darkies and I'll bet they are plenty hungry."

Mattie, a robust black slave girl about 25 years old, appeared from within the mansion. "Yessir, massa Tom. I bees fryin' dem chicken up directly." Looking directly at Tom's guests, Mattie said, "Doz y'all wants sum mo' dat sweet tea?" All the guests declined a refill.

All of the family, including the two cousins and the Robbins, sat at the large dining room table. It had been immaculately set and was being served by five of the house slave girls, who were all properly dressed in their uniforms. As one of the younger girls entered the room, Allie noticed that under her white tied belt was the doll which Allison had dropped on her first visit. This girl must have been the one who saw a ghost. She didn't recognize Allie, and she went on with her normal serving to the table.

After grace was said and the food was served, Tom began the table conversation. "Y'all gonna stay for a spell, aren't ya? We got plenty of plantation to show ya in the next couple of days." Tom's cousins were planning to leave the next morning. They had a long trip back to Virginia.

Tom was proud of his plantation and he wanted for his visiting reporters to be able to witness, firsthand, the activities that went on at the Greenwell plantation. Tom said to Daniel, his oldest son, "I want you and Bobby to fetch a buggy and take Mr. Marley 'round the property for a good close look at the goings on."

Daniel, begrudgingly, said "Why I gotta take that liberal minded brodder of mine? He ain't nothin 'cept a pain in the ass."

Tom replied in a rather stern voice, "You do what you're told, boy. I ain't 'lowing no squabbling twinx you two."

Sarah, Tom's wife, and Allison were sitting together at the far end of the table. They were becoming quite attached to each other. Sarah offered to show Allie around the house, the staff, the canning process, and all of the womanly functions of running the house. She also offered to allow Allie to watch as the slave girls prepared the food for the family. Baking chitlin and corn bread and properly spicing and cooking greens, field peas and the like was something that was a special talent, possessed only by finely trained servants. They were the only ones allowed to do the cooking. The other girls tended to housekeeping and serving the meals.

As the maid servant who had the voodoo doll in her apron came close, Allie asked where she had gotten it. "Dar be a ghoos dat visited," said the girl. "She musta drapped it cuz I seed it on de flo. It bees mine, sept it be lost ever since a nudder ghoos visit a whilst ago." Allie realized that she was referring to Nathan's visit previously. Time here seemed so different. It had been years since Nathan had made his appearance there. The girl referred to it as though it was just a few weeks ago.

Daniel Greenwell, who was quite an activist and always wanting to start a controversial discussion, said, "Them damn Yankees are still trying to stir up trouble for us Southerners. Now they wantin' ta make us give up our slaves. Let them come down and raise all their precious cotton and see who would have to do all the work. I ain't plowing dem fields or choppin' dat cotton."

Tom spoke up and told Daniel to keep his comments about political matters to himself. Their visitors were here to see the functioning of a plantation, not get bogged down in local political ideas. "Leave them damn Yankees alone for the time being," Tom said.

After dinner everyone was served a generous slice of fresh apple pie. Neither of the investigators had ever tasted pie as good. Allie told Sarah that she wanted the girls to teach her how to bake that way. "Tomorra I's gwin show ya all da cookin' I does," said Mattie, who appeared to be the head of all the house servants.

Marley noticed that all of the silverware, china, and crystal that they ate with was the same as he and Allison had found deserted in the old mansion. There was no comment about it, but there were many things that the visiting couple recognized, such as paintings and furniture.

When they were shown to their bedroom, they acted like they didn't know the way. The accommodations were excellent, except for the lack of a bathroom. They both settled in for a good night's sleep.

In the early hours of the morning they were awakened by the loud crowing of several roosters. The sun was just rising over the horizon and breakfast had already been prepared. Allison and Marley slipped back on the clothes they had on the day before and made their way down to the dining room for a hot morning meal. There were warmed over beans and cornbread, along with grits, bacon, fresh biscuits with homemade jam, and fried eggs. Now they realized why everyone was a bit overweight. Who could eat like this all the time?

After everyone had finished breakfast and the maids began cleaning up from the meal, there was a bit of time that allowed Allison and Marley to present the Greenwells with the small gifts that they had brought with them. The couple told the Greenwell family that they wanted to present some items to them and that they would like to meet back, in a few minutes, in the study where the presentations could be made.

Both of the visitors hurriedly went to their room and secured the gifts that they wanted to present. They went back down to the study, where they were met by the entire host family.

Marley started off, not to outdo Allie, but because men's business during those days always took precedence over women's concerns. He laid upon the table several small plastic zip lock bags. Just the sight of these bags astonished the observing family. They had never seen plastic, let alone self-sealing bags.

As Marley proceeded to open each of the bags, which were all labeled with the type of seeds that they possessed, he explained the value of each of them. When Tom Greenwell saw the corn seeds, which Marley had told him would produce much more and more healthy corn, he immediately secured them and gave them to Daniel and instructed him to have the darkies fence in a special two-acre tract where these seeds could be planted. This way they could keep a close eye on them and if they were much superior to their corn, they would save the produced seeds for planting the following year. "If these corn seeds do what you say they will do," said Tom to Marley, "we would have a much larger yield from our crop, even if grown on the same amount of land. We could easily increase our profits from this corn by a large bit. I won't know until next year when the harvest comes in if I should thank you."

Mr. Robbins explained about the various seeds that he had brought. Sarah Greenwell assured Marley that they would create a special test garden, up close to the house, for the planting of these other seeds. They were all excited about seeing the products that would be produced by planting these new hybrid seeds. They had to plant them close to the house to keep the cattle, yard animals, and deer from eating the tender sprouts.

After Marley finished, it was Allie's turn to make her presentations. She took out her bag that contained perfume, powder, and lipstick. When she opened the first bottle of French perfume, Sarah screeched with joy. Allie dabbed a little on her finger and placed it behind Sarah's ear. The wonderful fragrance filled the entire room. The visitor then took out some body powder and brushed it onto the face of her hostess. With a small amount of lipstick, used for rouge on her cheeks, and a little on her lips, Sarah's appearance was completely changed. Tom blurted out, "My God what a beautiful lady. And she's my wife."

Tom was asked if he approved of the changes that had been made to his wife. "Damn straight I approve. I ain't never seen her look that pretty nor smell that good. I can't wait for us to have company over so I can show her off." Tom added, "The governor and his wife are coming to visit next month, and I would appreciate it if Allie would show her how to make herself up that pretty. Everyone will be so very impressed. Shoot, she's prettier than a newborn mule."

After the presentations, Allison was led off to follow Sarah on a tour of the entire plantation home. She was shown the cooking area along with where the wood for the stove was stored. Outside the back door there was a large water trough where dishes were washed. Another trough stood beside the washing trough. This one was for storing drinking water. There was a path outside the back door that led about 50 feet to the living quarters for the house servants. Behind that was a small outhouse for use by the slaves. To the left, and more closely located to the big house, was a larger outhouse for the Greenwells and their guests.

There was a large chicken pen and coop where eggs were collected daily. There were also several free-range chickens running around the yard. In the corner of the pen was a tree stump that was used as a chopping block for removing the chickens' heads. Beside it was a large iron pot for scalding the dead chickens and removing their feathers.

Two black men were in a small field near the house plowing and planting the truck patch where the household vegetables and melons were to be grown. There was activity all around. Everyone had a specific job to do, and they were all busy doing that to which they were assigned. Sarah called out to the two black men and told them that she wanted a special garden placed up close to the main house to grow the new seeds that they had just received.

"Yes ma'am. We be comin' up there directly. We get rite on dat job fer ya," was called out by one of the men.

Daniel and Bobby pulled up to the front of the mansion with two horses attached to a small flatbed wagon. They had come to pick up Marley to take him on a tour of the plantation. One of the servants brought out a sealed jar of tea and six sandwiches. "Y'all gwin be gon fer a bit. Ya maw said y'all gwinna need som food fo y'all get bak." Bobby took the food and drink and secured it for the buggy ride, which in some places would be quite bumpy.

CHAPTER 6

Marley donned a large broad brimmed straw hat to prevent the sun from burning the back of his neck and shoulders, like it did on many of the farm and plantation workers, thus causing those who saw them to call them "red necks."

Before the buggy had gotten away from the mansion, Daniel and Bobby began arguing. Bobby was a small, frail young man while Daniel was much larger. Daniel usually ended up winning the arguments. They continued to argue most of the day as they traveled throughout the plantation. There were no large disputes. They just couldn't get along with each other. Marley recalled how it was suggested, based on findings at the mansion in much later years, that Daniel had killed Bobby and hid his body away behind the large fireplace. Now the motives of this murder seemed to becoming clear and understandable.

About a mile down the dusty road they came to their first stop. It was a row of about twenty-five very small shack cottages in a single row. Each of the houses had a small fireplace with a poorly constructed brick chimney. There was a small front porch on about 5 or 6 of the shacks. The porch was not elevated, it just protruded out from the house. The walls were all made of roughhewn wood planks, many of which did not fit together tightly, causing cracks to appear in the sides. The floors of all the shacks were dirt and there was only one room per house. The inside dimensions were about 12 X 14 feet and all the individual families had to make this space do as their living domain.

Outside of each cabin was a small area in which they could build a fire for cooking. Behind the shacks stood three fairly large outhouses, which were shared by all of the families. There were several black children who were running around outside the houses. All of the children were being supervised by two black women, who rotated their responsibilities each week. The women were needed more for working the fields than babysitting.

At the far end of the row of houses was a small vegetable garden which was fenced with split logs and leftover lumber. This garden was maintained by all of the slaves and it produced food that they all could share. The bigger the man of the family was, the larger share of vegetables his family would receive. There was never more than enough to go around, but it seemed adequate to feed them all.

The cabin row was located on about two acres of cleared land. About 50 feet behind the cabins was the beginning of large trees and an extensive forest. There were four mangy, skinny dogs that had free range of the property, along with about twenty-five chickens and two pigs. Although the housing situation was much less desirable than that of the plantation owners, it seemed to fairly well fit the basic needs of the residents. When asked how many slaves lived in these cottages, Bobby and Daniel again started a big argument. They just couldn't get along or agree on anything.

Marley and his guides made their way down the dusty road until they came to ten extremely large fields. These fields were well over 100 acres each. The Greenwell family had found that they could manage the cotton better if it were planted in 100 acre plots. In the off seasons they would allow the cattle to roam freely in the various fields. The cow's droppings provided excellent fertilizer for the following year's crop.

These fields were all planted with cotton and they were tended by several slaves. Now that the cotton plants were up and growing, the slaves had to constantly chop the cotton fields to keep the weeds out. Growing cotton appeared to be a continuous job, from the tilling of the soil to the planting of the seeds. From there the new plants had to be kept up and see that no weeds choked them out. After the cotton was mature, it had to be harvested, weighed, and sent to the gin. The old used plants would then be cut down and plowed into the soil to nourish it until the next planting season. It was no wonder that it took an army of workers to keep up with the entire process of raising cotton. Although many cotton fields were planted near a water source, there was rarely any irrigation to be worried about. Rain and mother nature were the only factors that were considered in enhancing the crops.

A couple of miles down the road the trio located several medium sized fields, each approximately 10 acres each. These fields were used for growing corn, soybean, squash, beans, and potatoes. One section, about an acre large, was set aside for watermelons. All of the crops that were not consumed by the plantation owners and their families were taken into the local towns and communities and sold at the market.

When the travelers reached an area where there were several slaves working a field, Daniel pulled their wagon to a stop. He got out and approached the workmen. "I want y'all to block off half of one of these 10-acre fields and prepare it specially for growing a special kind of corn," Daniel told them. "Y'all going to have to look out special for this field. We are gonna weigh the corn yield and compare it to the corn that we have been growing. I'll bring you the special corn seeds when it is close to planting time."

Daniel, Bobby, and Marley stopped along the way for the group to have lunch and something to drink. They stopped in an area with several large hardwood trees that provided welcomed shade. This was a favorite location for the Greenwell family to host picnics. It was extremely lovely and peacefully relaxing. There was a small creek that ran close to their picnicking area, which made this entire small location seem like an oasis in the middle of a desert.

After leaving the rest area, they headed further down the road. It gently curved and the three on the viewing expedition, the two horses, and small wagon were now headed back in the direction of home. Along the way they came to a large field on which there were about 80 cows and 2 bulls. There were also several goats, and in one corner there was a pig sty where there lived 12 large pigs and 8 small ones. As the group passed, they could almost identify the animals by the pungent odor that was emitted. Marley was told that these animals were raised for the family to eat. The plantation did not raise cattle for sale at the markets. When there was an excess of animals born, the Greenwells would share a couple with the slaves, who always held a large barn fire/cook out and all enjoyed the welcomed feast.

To the side of the cow field was a fair size barn where hay was stored and cattle were sheltered in the extremely cold weather, which was very seldom here in the south. Inside the barn lived three wild cats, which were kept there to keep the mouse residents in the corn crib at bay.

The wagon headed back to the main house where a big dinner meal was being prepared. Marley was ready to get off the wagon, get a big cool drink of tea, and get away from the constant bickering between Daniel and Bobby.

CHAPTER 7

When Marley stepped back onto the large front porch of the mansion, he was greeted with a tall cold mint julip. He and Tom sat on the porch and rocked as Tom questioned Marley about his day touring the plantation. They discussed the several things that the Greenwell boys had taken him to see. He assured Tom that he had gathered quite enough information to take back home and write an interesting article, perhaps even a full book.

When Marley saw Tom puffing on a big cigar, he rushed up to his room where he had left some fine Cuban cigars that he had brought for his host. He quickly returned to the porch and presented the cigars to Tom, who immediately unwrapped one and lit it up.

"Damn these cigars are smooth. What state grew this fine tobaccee?" asked Tom.

"This tobacco was grown and the cigars processed in Cuba," stated Marley. "They are in great demand by many gentlemen."

"I can certainly see why," stated Tom. Both men relaxed back in their rocking chairs, enjoying their bourbon drink and their fine cigars.

The crisp sounds of the farm bell rang loud enough for anyone within a mile to hear. Mattie called out, "Y'all bees commin. Dinna gwin be served directly and Miss Allison and me been working ponst it all day, and I is shor it gwin be fine."

The entire family gathered around the splendidly set table. Tom said grace and the servants began bringing in the food. There were two large pheasants on one plate and about 10 quail on another. Mashed potatoes, butter beans, and gravy were also served. In the middle of the table was a large hand sliced loaf of homemade bread. The meal was nothing less than a feast, but this was the type of meal that was served to the Greenwells every day.

As they all set around the table, Marley mentioned that he and Allison would be going home the following day.

Sarah and Tom let out a sigh. "We have really enjoyed your company," said Sarah to her visitors.

"We have thoroughly enjoyed our visit," stated Marley, "but we must go back home and begin compiling all of the notes that we have gathered here on the plantation. Allie and I both feel that we have brought gifts to you that will change your entire lives. If you plant the various seeds that I have brought, and if they produce abundantly as I have told you they would, you may want to share some of the future seeds with friends and neighbors. This will give us a great feeling of accomplishment for having brought you such products. Future generations will prosper from the great advancements that you will make with these crops."

Allison smiled at Marley and said, "I can't wait until you taste the dessert that Mattie and I made. It is bread pudding topped with bourbon sauce. It contains crushed pecans and some preserved peaches. Mattie says that it is one of her specialties."

After dinner, one of the slave girls came over to the Robbins. "I's gwin be up ta ya room directly to gather your'n dirtee clooz. Y'all haz dem sittin outside da room and I gwin wash dem and fetch dem rite back outside yo doo." Allie was pleased to know that they would have clean clothes to wear home the next day.

When they had finished their meal, they all headed to their separate bedrooms. Although it was only 8:30, everyone here got to bed early and rose up with the chickens. Back in their room, Marley asked Allie if she thought that she needed to write down any notes about their visit.

"I don't think so," she said. "I have been so impressed and excited that I don't think I could forget anything that I saw."

The slave girl, Edna, came to pick up the dirty clothes. While she was there, Allison took her aside and told her that she wanted her to do a big favor for them.

Edna said, "Yessum, Miss Allie. Massa Tom don tol us ta do anything y'all had a reconing fer."

Allie told Edna that this must be a strict secret between the two of them. Edna understood.

The next morning at 3 am, before anyone else got out of bed, Edna came to the Robbins' bedroom, woke them up, and delivered their clean clothes. She then led them downstairs and into the small room, through which they had originally come. This room had been closed to the rest of the family since Marley and Allison arrived. The stairway leading up to the closet was still in place. Edna simply led them to the door of the room, but she did not come in, nor did she look inside.

The reporters hurried to the stairs that were awaiting them, scampered upstairs and into the small closet in Nathan's room, where they secured the metal sphere which they had left there, and oriented the N away from north. A small rumble occurred, and the stairs were removed from leading down and the floor securely closed back. There was no trace of their venturing through time. Marley led Allison back out of the closet and into the bedroom. They placed the metal sphere back on the shelf, from wince it had been taken, and they both headed back to their own bedroom where they would sleep the rest of the night and wake in the morning to some fascinating discussions.

Back at the Greenwell plantation, the family arose to find that their visitors had already gone. Both Sarah and Tom said that they would have liked to wish them goodbye. When they questioned if anyone had seen them get up and leave in the early morning, there was no reply.

"I guess they are just like us," said Tom. "They hate long partings. I do wish them well with their reports about our plantation."

CHAPTER 8

In the morning when Allison and Marley awoke, they looked at each other as if to say, "What the hell just happened?" They both slipped on lounging clothes and headed down to the kitchen for their first cup of coffee.

"This has been an amazing adventure," said Allie, "if I am to believe what I recently observed."

Marley settled her down by mentioning that they had observed many mysteries while occupying this mansion. Why should this be any different?

Allie replied, "Everything else that we have observed has been factual and believable. There were bodies, graves, treasures, and even strange spirits, but there has never been something that we could not explain or understand. How do you think that we will be able to tell others about this time trip? No one will believe us unless we actually show it to them. If we don't show it, we will be the laughing stock of the history community, especially the professors."

After a long discussion, the two decided that they would not show anyone the time travel method that Nathan had discovered. Without telling that they'd actually been there, they would tell the details of how life existed in the 1850s. The fascinating part of this experience was that they could now tell the history and occurrences of an actual antebellum plantation. They could present the details just like they had actually been there, which they had. The details and observations that they would tell others would be so very accurate that everyone would wonder where they secured their information.

After breakfast, both of the reporters headed to their individual studies, where they secured paper and pen and began recording their own findings of their travels. Allison had pages to write about the functioning of the mansion, along with the slaves teaching her how to cook their own favorite dishes. Marley was more zoned in on writing about the physical attributes of the plantation. He was able to meet with several of the slave men and could report their feelings about their situation and how they were being treated. As Marley considered the ramifications of the entire visit, he came to the conclusion that it was best that he and Allie had returned home when they did. He did not want to enter into any conversations that were too detailed about the Greenwell's political feelings or what he had been questioning the slaves about. He had learned all that was needed, and it had been time for them to return home.

The word leaked out about the Robbins having new and interesting facts concerning the Greenwell mansion, along with information about the actual life on a Southern plantation. Marley and Allie were both invited to give lectures on several university campuses, as well as to several community service organizations. It was extremely difficult for these speakers to present their facts without disclosing that they had actually been there. They both decided upon a "what if" approach. They would start their lecture by stating, "What if you could actually visit a working plantation of the 1800s?" This way everyone could imagine that they had been present themselves.

The maintenance of Marley and Allison's secret was more than they could bear. They had to tell someone, or they would just explode. The couple had a dear friend who was the chairman of the history department at a university. He had written several books concerning the antebellum South. Besides being a close friend, he was someone that they could trust completely. An appointment was made for them to meet with him in his office.

The Robbins were both quite nervous about sharing their knowledge about their time travel, with him or with anyone. They did, however, manage to come clean with their story about visiting the old mansion. The facts were difficult for their friend, Dr. Ames, to understand. He knew these historians for many years, and they had always acted, thought, and reported in a logical, orderly manner. This was something quite different. Dr. Ames admitted that it was difficult for him to believe their outlandish story. He would, however, be happy to travel to their home and see the phenomenon for himself. This way he could either have the two committed to a nut farm or he could help them promote the evidence of their findings. Dr. Ames was an elderly professor who had been suffering for years with a bad heart. He was not about to tarnish his reputation by telling of something with which he was not personally familiar.

The Robbins decided to invite Dr. Ames to come to their home and they would show him their hard-to-believe findings. They required Dr. Ames to sign a legal statement that he would not disclose the details, nor the founders, of this discovery to anyone. He gladly signed the papers because he wanted to see this time travel device for himself.

CHAPTER 9

The day finally arrived for Dr. Ames' visit to the finely restored mansion where Marley and Allison resided. He was graciously greeted at the door and shown to the kitchen, where they all sat and had a cup of coffee.

Dr. Ames began the conversation by saying, "You two are my closest and dearest friends. I would like to share something with you that is very private for me. I have been told by my doctors that I only have a couple of months to live. My heart is rapidly giving out."

Allie gasped and said, "Tell us that isn't the truth."

Dr. Ames assured them that he was correct about his diagnosis. He said, "If your story is correct, I want to see the facts before I die. There will be plenty of historians after I am gone, but I want to see something that will really knock my socks off so I can die without my boots on."

Marley explained the details about the time warp, even the facts that led up to their discovery. He told Dr. Ames about the metal sphere that had to be oriented toward the north for the entrance to the time warp to open.

Dr. Ames had one large request to make before they showed him the hidden closet and the stairway leading into the past. He wanted to descend the stairway by himself, unaccompanied by anyone. If he were to be allowed to view this astonishing phenomenon, he chose to do it by himself. Additionally, Dr. Ames wanted to be in possession of the metal sphere at all times.

Since there were no objections to his requests, Dr. Ames was led into the bedroom which was once occupied by Nathan Greenwell. The three secured the metal sphere and handed it to Dr. Ames. He had been instructed about turning the N on the sphere to face north.

When the doctor entered the small closet, he carefully oriented the N to face to the north. The floor began to rumble and an opening appeared, through which he could pass. Below the opening was a stairway that led to the lower room of the old Greenwell mansion. Dr. Ames could easily view servants and family members milling around in the adjacent rooms. The Robbins' story was true. It was just like they had reported.

Dr. Ames grasped the metal sphere securely, which appeared to be the object that activated the time warp. He headed, alone, down the stairway. Halfway down he looked back and called to Marley and Allison, "I now realize that all that you have told me is true. I have a very short time to live and since I have no family, I choose to live out my final days with those of whom I have studied and written."

As he reached the bottom step of the descent, he took the metal sphere and reoriented the N so that it would not point north. A rumbling again occurred, and the stairway disappeared. The access in the floor of the closet then became completely sealed up. There was no way that their friend could be rescued from the past. It was his desire. What better way to spend your final days then where and how you chose?

Marley called the local police and reported all of the details about his friend's disappearance. When the authorities arrived, they could find no evidence of any time travel device, nor could they find evidence that Dr. Ames had ever been there. They certainly did not believe the fantastic story that Marley and Allie told them. The entire case was swept under the rug and listed as a fanciful tale that had been told by two dreamer historians.

Back at the university, Dr. Ames had left a note on his desk. It read, "I have lived my life in search of history. Now that I have found it, I plan to spend my final days in its enjoyment."

Book Three:

Uncle Frank's Scary Stories

Uncle Frank's Scary Stories

Chapter One

Uncle Frank was an old black man whose heart was as pure as gold. He lived in a split log cottage down at the edge of town. Everyone loved Uncle Frank, as he chose to be referred to, for his outgoing gentleness and great compassion. The kids in the town loved him for his adventurous and mysterious character, as well as his great storytelling ability. He kept mostly to himself, but he loved to have the children of town come to his home, sit in front of the wood burning fireplace, and listen to his many tales of his younger days. No one could really tell the age of old Frank but judging from the deep furrows in his brow, the long lines in his face and neck, and the cotton white fringe of hair that bordered both sides and the back of his bald head, most children judged him to be about 200 years old.

He walked using an old bent cane, which he had made from a fallen limb. His back was hunched and there were seldom any shoes on his feet. Uncle Frank didn't appear to have any earthly possessions, except for his old briar pipe which was always lit and producing rings of pleasantly smelling smoke that circled his head as he walked. When at home, the sweet pipe odor filled his entire cabin.

The small cabin that he called home was only one room. It was, however, comfortable for Frank and he never complained about his living conditions. In one corner there was a wooden slat bed with a thin mattress. Against the main wall stood a fireplace, which warmed the cabin and provided for his cooking needs. There were a few handmade chairs and a simple wooden table that stood in the middle of the room. Behind the cottage stood a small out house. It was only 4 or 5 steps from the back door and often unpleasant odors found their way into his small cottage.

Frank split his own logs for burning in his fireplace. This was his only means of keeping warm and preparing meals. The split firewood stood in neat piles beside the outer walls of the cabin and on his small porch. In the yard there was a large iron pot which provided him with a wash tub for his weekly laundry.

This small unpretentious home was located about three miles down a dusty dirt road from the town itself. It sat on an acre of well-manicured rural property where its only neighbors were tall slender pine trees and some majestic old oaks. The oaks cast weird, frightening shadows when the moon was approaching full. At night the breeze through the swaying pines created an eerie sound that could be heard for many yards down the dark road. These characters, along with the fact that Frank's home was down an extremely dark road, was what kept many of the town's children from pursuing nightly visits to his cottage.

Often several children would gather and join to make a brave night trip to Uncle Frank's. They would always be carrying one or two kerosene lamps to help light their way, and heaven forbid, if Frank would tell them a scary story, the lamps would help light their way back home.

On one particularly gloomy, foggy night, four of the children gathered and planned their three-mile journey down the dark road. They were never guaranteed that they would ever return to their homes, but that was part of what made the encounter so invigorating and seemingly dangerous. Frank had been told of the four boy's visit that night and he was expecting the frightened group. He met them at the road, by the path that led to the cabin. Frank stood extremely still beside the major fence post that led into his yard. As the children passed him and proceeded up the path to his home, Frank stepped out and greeted them with a deep and unsettling "HELLO." The children all yelled and ran as fast as they could to the door of the cabin. One of them even wet himself on the way.

Uncle Frank had not meant to cause such a fright. He was just being friendly and welcoming his visitors. After they had all had a good chuckle, they filed into the cottage and found a comfortable spot to sit. Frank took his place at the foot of the fireplace, where he was comforted by the small flames and glowing embers of the hearth. His pipe had gone out, so he secured a small twig from the fire and brought it to the bowl. Three large puffs sufficiently lit his pipe again and the pleasant aroma began filling the room. Frank could see that the four young men that had come to visit were rather anxious about their surroundings, especially their walk home later that night. He took full advantage of the situation and leaned back on the wall and asked them if they would like for him to tell them a story of how old Miss Hattie got lost in the swamp and the only thing that was found was her pink bonnet and one shoe.

The children scooted closer to one another and they all agreed that they wanted to hear Frank's grizzly tale. One of the children stepped over to the wall and fetched another small log to place on the fire. He hoped that this would provide a little more light to illuminate the dark room. One could almost hear the teeth chatter from the four brave boys. Knees trembling and holding tight to one another, they nodded to Uncle Frank and motioned for him to begin his wild tale.

Chapter Two

"Well," Frank began in his deep, raspy country voice, "it was a night very much like this. The moon was almost full, but the night was dark because of the thick fog that filled the air. The large old oaks cast shadows onto the ground. The fog was so thick, you couldn't distinguish more than shapes, not even identify what type of animal made them. Miss Hattie took her dog and headed down the dark road toward the town. She needed some bread and a few fresh eggs. Hattie knew that the market was closed but she also knew the owners and could persuade them to open and serve her. There were no lights, either on the road or in the town which lay ahead.

Hattie had made this trip several times before in the dark. The only thing that she feared were the several snakes that crawled into the road from the swamp which was adjacent to the dirt road. She figured that her dog would certainly alarm her if there was any pending danger. Miss Hattie had figured wrong. Halfway down the road a barred owl hooted out its eight distinctive hoots. It swooped down and latched onto the back of Hattie's dog. A death-defying pursuit then followed. There was hair and feathers flying everywhere. The dog tried to bite the owl and the owl just held on for dear life. The dog let out a blood curdling holler as he broke loose from the talons of the massive owl. He then took off back home at a full speed run. Hattie was left all alone. Should she turn back, or should she continue her trip to town? The fog was beginning to lift a bit and she could see a reflection of the moon in the still swamp water. This reflection provided her with a little light, so she decided to continue on her journey.

The light of the moon shone upon the eyes of the several alligators that swam in the swamp. This light created an eerie glow of red eyes. Hattie was not bothered by the alligator eyes for she had seen this sight before. What did bother her were the two sets of larger eyes that glowed from about 10 feet up in the trees. She knew that the moon did not cause a red reflection from the eyes of other animals. What could they be? As quickly as they appeared, the eyes disappeared. This only left unsettling thoughts to bounce around in Hattie's imagination.

"Where the hell is my dog when I need him," Hattie screamed. She looked again into the marshy waters and she could see that the piercing red eyes of the alligators were coming closer to her. Down the road Hattie ran at full speed, hoping that the lights of town would soon come into view. As she looked up toward town, she stumbled on a broken limb and fell flat on her face in the mud. As she struggled to get up her hand grabbed something nearby, which turned out to be a full-grown water moccasin. She quickly slung the snake as far as she could. Looking closely, she found that she had suffered no bites, only a few scratches from her fall.

Our lady traveler sat in the stillness of the night and began to sob. She didn't know what to do. As she placed her head, face down, into her hands she heard a whining sound that sounded like it was coming from the swamp. She looked up just in time to see the two sets of glowing red eyes, high in the trees, coming directly toward her. Stumbling to her feet, Hattie began to run back in the direction of her house. After four or five large steps, she heard the hissing of an alligator. Looking up she could see its menacing glowing eyes directly in front of her. The gator had crawled into the road and blocked her progress. Turning around, she found that another alligator had entered the road right behind her. Her way was blocked. Hattie's only hope to escape these two monsters was to head directly into the murky waters of the swamp. She realized that she would be faced with other gators and poisonous snakes if she entered the water, but this was the only choice she had.

After wading into the water until it was up to her thighs, she began to make her way back in the direction of her home. She trudged through the grasses and her feet felt strange objects as she walked through the muck. Was all of this terror just in her imagination or was it really true?

Hattie became extremely tired from her tedious journey through the swamp. There was a large cypress knee close by where she decided to take a short rest. Through the moonlight, she could see that there was a large snake which was occupying the flattened surface of the knee. She grabbed a large fallen stick and shooed the snake away from its perch. Knowing that the snake was still in the general area, Hattie used extreme caution when approaching the resting spot.

After sitting for about two minutes, exhaustion overcame her and Hattie drifted off to sleep. She quickly awoke when a sharp pain pierced her lower leg. The snake must have returned. Opening her eyes, she glanced up into the adjacent trees. There staring down upon her were the two large pair of glaring red eyes. Hattie let out a scream loud enough to be heard for a mile. The noise of the scream must have roused the alligators for the piercing eyes of these vicious animals were heading directly toward her.

The next morning when Hattie was reported missing, a bloodhound was used to trace her into the swamp. Once there, the only things that could be found were her bonnet and one of her shoes. There was no blood, no bones, and no other clues.

"I suppose," continued old Uncle Frank, "that what go on in the swamp amongst those critters is just meant to stay there."

When Frank finished with his story he turned back to the fireplace and knocked out the ashes from his pipe. "I reckon it's 'bout you young'un's bedtime. Your mammy and pappy is g'win' to be worrying 'bout y'all," Frank told the boys.

Although they were hesitant about going out into the dark night, they all knew that they had better be getting home. They quickly made their way down the path to the dirt road. When they hit the road, they all set out in a full gallop toward their homes. No one wanted to be left behind to face the spooky shadows of the giant old oak trees.

As a matter of fact, the four youngsters reached their homes in record time. They were all sweaty and breathing hard. They all told their parents that they had a race all the way home. Since it was Saturday night, the boys all rushed off to bed knowing that they had to rise early, bathe, and get ready for church the next morning. None of them spoke a word about their visit to Uncle Frank's or the scary tale that he had told them. They knew that their parents often frowned upon their nighttime visits down the dark and deserted road.

Chapter Three

The next afternoon, after church and dinner, the four brave explorers wandered down the road toward Frank's cottage. They had no intention of stopping but they did want to give their friend a friendly wave. They could even set up another evening meeting and have old Uncle Frank tell them another tale.

Frank was out behind his shack and he was digging with a small, makeshift shovel. The boys could see that he had dug two or three shallow holes in his backyard. They hid behind a large bush and continued to watch as Frank dug. Each time he would move on to another digging location, he would utter a few choice words which indicated his frustration. He never retrieved anything from the holes he dug but he kept on digging. Soon Frank was completely tuckered out. He covered up the small holes and headed back into his cabin to get a drink of water and rest his tired back.

The inquisitive boys could not stand not knowing exactly what their elderly friend was up to. After the old gent got back into the house, the boys quietly eased their way down the front path and onto Frank's small porch.

"Is you there," called out Billy Ray. He was a year older than the other boys and he thought that he should be their leader.

"Sho I is here," Frank called back. "Where y'all pickneys think I g'wan' be? Come on in."

As they opened the front door, the boys could see that Uncle Frank was stretched out on his wood slat bed and covered with some ragged clothes. His fireplace contained a modest fire and his pipe sat on the shelf of the hearth.

"What you young'uns doin' down in my neck of the woods?"

Billy Ray said that they were just taking a stroll and happened up onto his cabin.

Tommy Jo, the youngest of the group, said that they were curious as to what he was digging for in his back yard. The other boys seemed to be quite embarrassed, but they were ready and willing to listen to any explanation that Frank may have.

"Well, ya see," began Uncle Frank, "dat is a long story and I spec that I may need another evening of y'all visiting to tell you the whole thing."

The young men agreed to come back in a couple of days for Frank to fill them in on the complete story. All he told them was that it was very eerie and it involved the widow Maggie Pemberton and her lost jewelry and gold. Most people thought that Mrs. Pemberton was a witch and she had killed her husband and took his money. Others said that her grotesque appearance had nothing to do with witchery. It wasn't her fault that she crawled around on all fours, or that she had no teeth and a large gnarly proboscis. Just because she was extremely ugly, it had nothing to do with her husband's death or the disappearance of her fortune.

141

"Now y'all scoot along back home, ya hear," said old Uncle Frank. "I'll fill y'all in when you come back to visit."

Several days later the boys gathered and made plans to sneak off to Uncle Frank's cabin. They had to leave after dark so no one would see where they had gone. Hating to travel the dark road at night, they made sure that they had a full can of oil to keep their night lamp burning. After sunset, the boys began to make bird whistles to one another, indicating that they were all ready to make their journey. They met up down by the schoolyard and together they set off towards Frank's house.

When they arrived, Uncle Frank was waiting on the porch. He was puffing away at his old pipe, which he had just filled with "rabbit tobacce." Although the smell wasn't as pleasant as his usual tobacco, the boys were happy to just smell the aroma of his pipe and know that he was there with them.

They all headed inside where each boy took up his regular listening place on the wooden floor. Frank slowly moved over to the fireplace and, grimacing with back pain, took his seat and enjoyed a few drags from his old pipe. The smoke, as he exhaled it from his mouth, made weird forms and cast spooky shadows onto the walls of the lodge. The boys all huddled together as close as possible to hear the story which was about to be related to them by Uncle Frank.

"Ya know that the devil haunts a hungry man," began the old man. "I ain't saying that Mr. Pemberton was so very hungry, but he sho had to put up with a lot of devil during his life. First off, Mrs. Maggie would most times make him sleep outside with his old yellow dog. They would sleep in an old split hollow log just outside the house. Sometimes the old dog would wake him up howling at a coon or the approach of a poisonous snake. Some folks said that that old dog was part rattlesnake. No matter, he was good for Mr. Pemberton by keeping away all the harmful critters. Although people round abouts all knew of the jewelry and riches that the Pembertons kept, no one was brave enough to approach them and try to find it.

"Mrs. Pemberton had an old, mean black cat with two piercing green eyes and claws as big as a rattlesnake's tooth. Some folks say that they saw the cat drinking the blood from a recently killed possum. I tell ya there is nothin' worse than tasting a possum's blood. The cat would prowl around their homestead causing fear to come to anyone who approached. Folks were more scared of that cat than they were of Mr. Pemberton's dog.

"Sometimes, late at night, there were greedy folks that tried to sneak up on the Pemberton house. The dog most never moved a muscle. Dat cat, however, would jump out from the shadows and claw and bite the intruders. There was one man who lived down in town that lost one eye and part of his right ear from that mean cat. The man would never say what he was doing out there in the first place.

"Behind Mrs. Maggie's house was an old, dilapidated barn. No one much entered the barn because it was chocked full of spiders, rats and snakes. The hinges of the barn had a terrible squeaking to them, like the sound of a casket being opened after it had been buried for several years. It was bad enough to try to go in there during the day, but it was impossible to approach it after dark. If the snakes and spiders didn't get you, surely you would be attacked by Maggie's mean black cat.

"It was said that the Pembertons hid their expensive possessions out there in the barn. It was also said that Maggie Pemberton, after she had killed her husband, took the valuables and hid them in holes that she dug around the property. No one really knew. There were only gossip tales going round and none of them led anywhere.

"One day, several years ago," continued old Frank, "I gots me up the courage to stroll on over to the Pemberton place. There was no trace of Mr. Pemberton, but through a crack in the wall I could make out the figure of Maggie Pemberton. She was down on the floor and crawling around on all fours, like she did most all the time. When she turned toward me I could see that there was blood coming out of her mouth. In one hand she held a large kitchen knife. From the corner of her mouth was the remains of the black tail of her old mean cat. On the floor were pieces of the dissected cat which still had blood dripping from them. As Maggie turned and faced my direction, I could see one of her eyes dangling down on her face. Beside her eyebrow was a long, newly placed, scratch mark. Obviously, her cat had scratched her eye out and Maggie killed and ate the cat as her form of punishment.

"I could feel the blood rush out of my face as I stood there in horror. 'Feet take me where I ain't,' I yelled as I turned to escape. I ran so fast, trying to get away, that I probably left my shadow yards behind me. Crashing through the bushes and briar patches, I rapidly made my way back to my house where I promised myself that I would remain and never venture to the Pemberton's again. No one ever saw Mr. or Mrs. Pemberton, his yellow dog or her mean black cat, ever again."

Uncle Frank, appearing to be worn out from the day's work, and now staying up telling ghost stories to the boys, leaned back on the fireplace and closed his eyes to rest.

Tommy Jo, in his excitement and intrigue, shouted out, "You ain't going to stop the story there, is ya?"

Frank had opened his eyes and stared directly into Tommy Jo's face. "Be patient now boy. I's g'win' tell you the whole story iffin ya jus' give me time."

Chapter Four

Uncle Frank could see that the boys were all frightened by the tale he was telling them. He decided to take it one step further.

"Nobody really knows if Maggie Pemberton is still alive. It's been said that her ghost is often seen crawling around their homestead. I believe that the treasure of the Pembertons is still buried either on their property or somewhere in their old barn. Their property isn't very far from here. Would you boys like to go up there and search for all that jewelry? I could go with you and hold one of the lanterns while y'all thoroughly search the barn."

One could readily see the paleness and fear entering the faces of the brave adventurers.

"You mean you want for us to go up to that haunted house and barn?" one of the boys asked.

"Surely you are not afraid of going up there tonight, are you?" queried Uncle Frank.

"No sir. We ain't scared. We just gotta know what exactly we are looking for," was the reply.

"I don't know exactly what you will be looking for," answered Frank. "I do know what you don't want to be looking for and I hope that you don't find it. Trouble has always come from that area and I hope you can find a way to avoid it tonight."

The four skeptical boys, along with Uncle Frank, grabbed an oil filled torch and a couple of oil lanterns. Together they exited the cottage and headed in the direction of the Pemberton estate. Two of the boys had to go to the bathroom but they were too frightened to be caught lagging behind. They just had to hold it, or maybe something would scare it out of them.

After about 30 minutes of hiking, the group finally reached the fence that gated the Pemberton property. From the edge of the fence, they could see the old farmhouse and a sagging old barn in the back yard.

"Come on," said Frank. "Just watch that you don't step on a snake or get caught in a spider's web. Black widow spiders are all throughout these woods, along with several types of poisonous snakes."

As they approached the farmhouse, the boys continued to recall how Frank had told them of Mrs. Pemberton eating her cat in the kitchen. As they got closer, their forward progress slowed.

"Are you sure that we want to do this?" questioned Billy Ray. "My mother told me to be home before it got too late."

Frank responded that it would only take a few more minutes if they were lucky. "You two boys go inspect the barn while me and the other two go through the house," ordered Frank.

"Maybe we should all stick together," suggested Tommy Jo. "That way we can all run at the same time."

Frank agreed that they could all stay together.

"You know we don't know if Mrs. Pemberton is still alive," came a soft voice from the back of the pack. "She might jump out and eat us just like she ate her cat."

Uncle Frank responded that it would be very unlikely that she is still alive, but it was suggested that they all keep their eyes open for any strange sounds or movements.

As the group entered the kitchen of the deserted house, they found the bones of a cat, dry and white, lying on the floor. The boys realized that Frank's tale must have been true. They held the lit torch up high so the most illumination possible could be produced. Slowly they all walked from room to room as they searched each area for traces of a hidden treasure. The boards creaked beneath their feet and the musty odor of stale air filled all of the rooms.

One of the adventurers stated that he got a whiff of rotting flesh. This statement was very unsettling to all of the others. As they entered into what appeared to be a bedroom they gathered around while one person held the torch and another slowly opened the closet door. From on top of a shelf in the closet, fell the body of a rotting racoon that had become trapped inside. This was apparently the source of the smell of rotting flesh.

The brave crew, having explored the entire house and finding nothing of value, moved cautiously out to the barn. The door was opened and sure enough there was the eerie sound of rusted metal against metal. The hinges of the barn doors had not been opened for years. The spooky sound did anything but relax the adventurers. They all began huddling closer to each other.

Uncle Frank was smart enough to break off a large twig from a bush outside the barn. He used this branch to swat away the spider webs, and possible spiders. No one cared what kind of spiders they were, the boys didn't want anything to do with them. As Frank frantically swatted around and removed the many webs, a few of the spiders were knocked off and they came landing on the boys. Each of the young men kept busy swatting each other and making sure that there were no spiders left.

After they all got completely into the barn, they heard a shrilled sound that came from up in the hay loft. From the area of the squeaking noise, the boys could see small drips of blood dripping through the rafters. Hank Jr., who was as goofy as he was brave, grabbed a lantern and begin climbing the ladder up to the loft. As he got to the top, he saw the back of a big black cat as it jumped over a bale of hay. Looking down where the cat had been, Hank saw a large dead rat. Obviously, the cat had just killed the rat and Hank ran the cat off. Hank picked up the dead rat by its tail and slung it down to where the other boys stood. A loud scream burst forth from the boys on the bottom floor.

"Come on boys," Hank called out. "It's only a dead rat."

When the boy in the loft moved toward the ladder which he had used to get up there, he encountered some loose boards where he stepped. He grabbed one of the boards and lifted it. He then lifted his light source so that he could see under the loose board. There, in the space between the floor of the loft and the ceiling of the under room, was the white, dried bones of a man. Hank called down to Frank and told him to come on up and see what he had found.

None of the boys wanted to be left alone so they all went up to the loft to see Hank's discovery. Upon examination, the bones appeared to be of a tall man. There was still a gold wedding band on his left hand. Frank removed the ring and read the inscription on the inside. J.P. was printed in bold letters.

"Josh Pemberton," Frank exclaimed. "Dis musta been where the old widow hid his body after she killed him."

They placed the board back over the bones and all went back down the ladder. "I reckon we done found enough for one night," said Uncle Frank. "Let's head back to my cabin."

The boys were all too happy to comply. At a fairly rapid pace the group of five headed back to the narrow dirt road that led back to Frank's home. They then all scampered down the road and quickly reached the cottage where Frank had left the fireplace burning.

"Sho is a welkum site," old Frank shouted out. "Y'all come on in and have a drink of water."

"No thanks," answered Billie Ray. "We dun had enough excitement for one night."

As Uncle Frank made his way back into his cabin, the four boys scurried back toward their homes.

"We ain't never going back there," said Tommy Jo.

"No. Not till the next time," claimed Hank.

Chapter Five

It was a couple of weeks before the adventuresome boys got up enough courage to go back to Uncle Frank's cottage and listen to more spooky tales. They went over in their minds what would be in the next tales that their old friend would tell them. Hopefully, the next story would be less gruesome. Perhaps they could even muster enough nerve not to be afraid to travel home at night, but what would be the fun in that?

Fairly early one Friday afternoon, about 3pm, the boys arrived at Frank's cabin. This time they were carrying shovels, pickaxes, lanterns, and a couple of baseball bats for protection. When Frank saw the young boys coming down the lane, he called out to them.

"Where is y'all headed? Looks like ya g'win' plant a garden or maybe search for buried treasure. Don't tell me y'all is hankering to go back to the Pemberton place again and look for that hidden gold and jewelry."

When they reached the porch of Uncle Frank's home, Billy Ray spoke up., "We decided we ain't scared of no old bones. They ain't no such thing as ghosts, so we ain't worried about that. We don't like spiders and snakes so we decided to come a little early so we wouldn't have to be there after dark. We want to see what we are dealing with."

Frank's eyes lit up because he was certain that anyone really searching for the treasure would be able to find it. He grabbed a lantern and an old, crooked walking cane and headed off with the boys on another exploration. It sure felt good knowing that his friends were not as frightened as they once were about this spooky situation.

It took less than half of an hour for the team to reach the Pemberton property. They went directly into the barn where they had found Mr. Pemberton's bones. Frank divided the team into two groups so they could cover more area. Bales of old hay were moved and shovels used to dig up the dirt floor.

Billy Ray and Hank went up into the loft to begin their search. They found several snakes, a few rotten eggs, and many rats. Their imagination wandered to what might have been there when they were there in the dark, several weeks ago. Thank goodness they couldn't see all the dangers and potential problems. Hank used his shovel to cut off the heads of several of the snakes. The rats moved too fast, but the feral cats were right on their trails. Billy Ray used a pickax to pull away some of the boards. Many of them were rotten and fell off without much effort on his part. Search as they would, nothing was to be found.

The boys on the upper level headed back down to join the boys and Frank on the lower level. They had been digging frantically, however, nothing was found. Soon the team became exhausted and decided to take a rest and get a drink of the water that they had brought. One of the boys climbed onto a railing that divided the barn into rooms. The railing sank about a foot and released a trap door that was hidden in the back wall. Tommy Jo and Hank rushed over to the door to examine what was behind it. There was a small room, but it was too dark to see anything inside. Billy Ray brought a lantern over to the hidden room. They lit it and held it up high so they could see into the mysterious room.

It was found that the room was very small, only about 5 feet by 6 feet. There was a piece of old cloth that was draped from floor to ceiling in one half of the compartment. Hank, being the brave explorer that he was, rushed into the small room and tore down the curtain. The two boys that had entered the room jumped back from freight. There, laying behind the curtain, were the bones and decomposed dress of Mrs. Pemberton. She was clutching a large kitchen knife. Her body had been in an upright sitting position but actions of the local rats had displaced many of her bones.

Frank and the other boys came running when they heard the shouts of the boys in the room. They all took a look at the death site of the old lady. There was nothing to do but to replace the veil and close the room back up, as they had found it. No one wanted to bother the bones or do any digging in this spooky room.

Tommy Jo said, "I'll bet the treasure is buried under the body of old Miss Pemberton. Maybe we should dig there." Everyone else thought that this was a bad idea and none of them pursued Tommy Jo's thoughts.

The sun was beginning to set and the small team of explorers closed up the barn and headed back to Uncle Frank's. They were all dejected because they had found no treasure, but they were also fulfilled by the several findings they made while searching through the intriguing, but scary, Pemberton property.

As the young men headed home after their visit at Frank's cottage, it had become completely dark. The shadows that were created by the oil lanterns that the boys carried made eerie images along the dusty road. All of the adventurers were frightened, but none of them wanted to let on. After about half of the way back home, Tommy Jo claimed that he saw a wild looking black cat following them. The boys' paces picked up as none of them wanted to prove Tommy correct in his observations.

Within 50 yards of the first boy's house, the group heard a distinct screaming sound, coming from deep within the wooded area around the house.

"That sounded like a wild cat, or maybe a bobcat," claimed Hank. "Who wants to go with me to check out the weird noise?"

There was no sign of participation from any of the brave young men. They were all anxious to reach their individual homes and climb safely into bed.

Chapter Six

One day, about a month later, old Uncle Frank came sauntering into town. He didn't have any shoes on his feet and he was puffing away at his old gnarly pipe. The smoke from the pipe circled his head and then drifted back behind him as though it was marking his trail. Frank was dressed in his old, tattered overalls and he was accompanied by an old yellow dog. His four friends met him as he came into town.

"Where did ya get that old mangy hound?" asked one of the lads.

"I reckon he just wandered up to my cabin one day," was Frank's answer. "He sure do look mangy and scrawny, ain't that the truth."

Uncle Frank proceeded to tell the boys about his recent adventure up to the Pemberton's property. He had gone there alone in hopes that he might find some clues about the lost fortune that was supposedly hidden there. The boys couldn't believe that he had gathered the nerve to go up to the property all alone. Immediately they began querying him about his adventure.

"Well sir," said Frank. "Ya'll know that der were nothin' good up there, 'specially in dat barn. All I could find was this old yellow dog, who proceeded to follow me home. I couldn't jus' let him starve, so I let him stay. I don't know if he was the Pemberton's dog but I sho do hope he ain't kin to that mean black cat."

All of the boys got a chuckle out of Frank's tale.

They followed Frank up to the general store where he bought some flour, two slabs of bacon, and some cooking lard. He also added in some salt and a stick of hard candy for each of the boys. They all strolled over and sat down on a bench that was outside the courthouse.

As they sat there discussing their adventures, two old, bearded men stumbled up to where they were. Neither of the men had any front teeth and one of them had a large scar on his forehead. They were crudely dressed and one of them wore an old straw hat, pulled way down over his eyes. They smelled like they hadn't bathed in weeks. When they stared at the group of young men and Frank, the boys saw that the men's squinting eyes were bloodshot.

One of the men stepped up and said in a grumpy, raspy voice, "We heared y'all been snooping round the old Pemberton place. Dar ain't nothin' out dar fer no pesky kids and no old man. Y'all best be keeping clear of that property lessen y'all wantin' to run into some real trouble."

When the straw hat was removed from the one man, the boys could see that one of his eyes had been ripped out and there were cat scratch marks on the rest of his face.

"We ain't trying to cause no trouble but iffin y'all go back out there, there will be the devil to pay," said the eyeless man. "Whatever is out there belongs to us and no one else. We g'win' be keepin' a close eye on the whole property."

"Y'all best be keepin quiet about anything you seed out there. Anyone else finds out about the property and your findings, we is coming back after you."

These grubby old men didn't have to tell our explorers twice about keeping their secret. They had already instilled the fear of the devil in them and that was all that was needed, or so thought the two evil looking men. As soon as they left, the boys and Uncle Frank began pondering exactly what was going on out at that old mysterious farm. Was there really a treasure hidden out there? Where could it be? The team had searched most everywhere that the loot could have been hidden.

Tommy Jo spoke up. "I told y'all that we should have dug under the bones of old Mrs. Pemberton. I'll bet those two men were too afraid to dig there, even if they had found the burial site. We oughta set out tomorrow night and do some more digging."

"How in the blue blazes do you spect to get up there without tipping off those two bad guys?" Billy Ray asked.

Uncle Frank piped in and said, "Why don't y'all come up to my cabin 'bout midday tomorrow. I'll have some coffee brewing and ya can smoke some rabbit tobacce. We'll make our plans for the dig then. We won't go up to the Pemberton place till after it turns dark outside so no one will know what we is up to."

LeRoy spoke up and said that his paw had two oil lanterns that he could bring.

"Never mind a bunch of lanterns," said Frank. "We can't be making much light and noise when we is up there."

Tommy Jo said in a muffled, frightened voice, "You mean we going up there in the dark?"

Frank said that he reckoned so. All that the boys needed to bring was a couple shovels, a pickax and some baseball bats for protection.

The young men looked excited, but in a very reserved way. They didn't know if the fear or the intrigue was the strongest driving force behind their explorations. They all broke up and went to their various homes for they realized that the next day would bring both exhaustion and fright. It was all in the game and they were all willing to participate.

The following day the boys all headed down the little unpaved lane to Uncle Frank's cottage, where they planned to spend the entire afternoon making plans. Once at the cottage, all the group took turns watching out for any sight of the two old evil men that they encountered in town. Since there was no sign of them, the expedition continued with their plans for the night dig.

The night sky was lit up with a full moon. Uncle Frank was to go first, carrying an oil lantern that was turned to its lowest brightness. After that was the crew of four young men, carrying a shovel, a pick, and three baseball bats. It was dark under the trees and some of the boys stumbled on the underbrush. They couldn't call out for help because they were to keep complete silence. The only thing that they could do was to get untangled and try to catch up with the other lads. This stumbling and fumbling continued until at last they saw Frank's lantern being waved up high in the air. This was the sign that they were to come meet him.

Once reunited, the group proceeded to the Pemberton barn. They went inside and found their way to where Mrs. Pemberton was buried. It was easy to find their way now since they had done this once before.

The small room that housed the Pemberton remains was barely large enough for all of the explorers to enter at one time. They all, however, wanted to stick together and not be left alone. Their one lantern must be used for lighting the area in which they were to dig, so anyone left outside the room would be left in the dark.

After carefully removing the shroud that divided the room, they gently moved the remaining bones to the side so they could begin digging. Digging down about a foot, they hit a hard object. They then took their axe and pried the hard box from the ground. Everyone held their breath, knowing that this was certainly the fortune that was left from the Pemberton riches.

There was a small lock that kept the box closed. The axe was used to knock off the lock. Uncle Frank held the lantern up high so they could all see in the box as it was opened. There in the box lay 20 large American gold coins. Also present was a gold and diamond necklace, two gold rings and a gold hair pin. This was all that was in the box, but the contents would add up to about $600 to

$1,000. They whooped because they thought that they were rich.

Just then the small door leading into the burial room was roughly and suddenly torn open. There in the light of their two lanterns stood the two frightful men that had approached them in town. Both of them had very grimacing looks on their faces. Without a word, they grabbed LeRoy, who was closest to the door, and held a knife to his throat.

"Give me the box and the loot," shouted the one-eyed man. "We told y'all that there would be trouble if ya came back out this way. Thanks for finding the treasure for us. We been looking for a long time."

The other man, who was holding LeRoy with a knife to his throat, said, "Now how can we make you boys and old man remember not to tell anyone about us or your discovery? I got me a big idea."

He jerked LeRoy around and quickly sliced off his right ear. Blood splattered everywhere as LeRoy grabbed for his missing ear.

"Y'all jus rememba what we is capable of doing to you, iffin you talk with anyone. We g'win' be watching you all de time."

The two men, along with the treasure and the box, quickly disappeared from the barn and completely out of sight. Uncle Frank turned up his oil lamp so it would produce more light. He tore off a strap from his overalls and tied it around LeRoys' head. A large handkerchief was used to put under the strap to protect the area of the missing ear and to stop the bleeding.

They all headed back out of the barn and went directly to Uncle Frank's house. There they washed LeRoy's wounds and put on a better dressing. They made up a story that the boys had been playing by a split wood fence and LeRoy fell off and caught his ear. The fall tore LeRoys ear plumb off and the boys put a dressing on it to stop the bleeding.

When the entire group had settled down and recomposed themselves, the boys headed back to their homes. There were a lot of tales to be told, but none about the actual happenings of that night.

Two or three times, on later occasions, the boys noticed the two gruff men hanging around in town. Most of the time they were drunk, but never did they appear to have taken a bath. They did wear some new shoes and new britches, but no one ever spoke with them nor inquired of where they had gotten the money for the clothes. Perhaps it would remain a mystery forever.

Chapter Seven

It was late in October and Halloween was just around the corner. Everyone was decorating their houses and yards and all of the children were preparing the costumes that they were going to wear while trick-or-treating. The big bad four, as our explorers liked to be called, were all planning to dress as ghosts. Each one would have a different type of costume, but they would all represent ghosts. For some reason, the lads enjoyed the macabre. Maybe it was from their experiences with Uncle Frank.

The boys all went down to Frank's cabin and asked him if he was going to come to town and go with them to get some goodies. Everyone would be handing out candies and other treats. Uncle Frank told the group that he was too old for running around the town and begging for treats. His plan was to stay in, pick a couple of pumpkins and carve them up with scary faces. He would then light them up with a candle and put them out on his porch. The boys were all welcome to come down to Frank's after they had finished their partying. He reminded them that it would be well after dark and the goblins may be out and running free on the dusty road leading to his cabin.

The big bad four had already been exposed to as much horror as Frank could dish out, or so they thought. On Halloween night the youngsters headed off to Uncle Frank's place. They knew that he would have the jack-o-lanterns lit up to try to scare them, but that didn't matter to these seasoned explorers. They headed off to meet with Frank anyway.

About halfway down to Frank's cottage was the town's cemetery. People had been buried there since 1824. There were no large headstones, just small, simple stones with names and dates inscribed in them. Two of the boys, LeRoy and Billy Ray, had grandparents that were buried in the yard. Their graves were well marked and often the boys would go there and place some wildflowers. There was a white picket fence that circled the graveyard, and no one ventured into the area after sundown.

You couldn't say that the gravesites were haunted, but several people had strange things happen to them when they went in at night. Three old ladies who went into the fence at night claimed that they saw strange movements in the bushes, and they heard weird sounds coming from some of the gravesites. One even claimed that she had seen an ugly, shaggy black cat which tried to scratch her. None of these people had any evidence and they could only rely on the others' word.

Late in the evenings, especially in late September, October, and November, many townsfolk claimed that they could hear moaning and cries for help coming from the direction of the cemetery. No one was brave enough to go and see where the sounds were coming from.

This being the end of October, it was right in the middle of the time that strange noises and occurrences came from the graveyard. As the boys passed the white picket fence of the yard, they quickened their steps so as not to encounter any of the oddities.

As they neared the far end of the fence, they all heard a deep voice calling, "LEROY! Come and help me."

This could not have been just in their minds because all four of the boys heard the voice. They paused in the dusty road and looked back, but nothing could be seen.

LeRoy called back, "Who are you and what do you want?"

The deep voice replied, "I need you to help me."

By this time all four of the boys felt quite uneasy with the strange voice. They urged LeRoy to come on and go to Uncle Frank's house. Tommy Jo even suggested that they leave in a dead run so as not to disturb any of the other cemetery residents. Hank, the brave but not too bright one, suggested that they all join LeRoy in finding out exactly who was calling him, and what he wanted.

It was true that all four of the lads were nervous, but their inquisitive minds drove them on. There was only one oil lamp among them, so LeRoy took it and headed back to the gate that led into the graveyard. Once inside the yard, all of the boys huddled together. This is the first time that they had been on a mystery mission without Uncle Frank along to help protect them.

LeRoy knew exactly where his grandfather had been buried and he went directly to the grave. He held the lamp up high so they all could see. Nothing seemed to be out of place. LeRoy called out several times for the voice to speak to them again, but nothing was heard. Tommy Jo again suggested that they all hurry along to Frank's and get out of the dark cemetery. They all agreed and headed out of the area. They closed the white fence behind them. As they walked away, they heard the creaking of hinges behind them. Looking back, they saw that the fence gate had been reopened, but no one was there.

The shrilled cry of a bobcat came from the trees on the far side of the graves. After that there were several hoots of an owl that was obviously close by. LeRoy held the lamp up high and caught sight of the golden eyes of a large owl in the trees above them.

"Perhaps it was only the call of the owl that we heard," said Billy Ray.

"Naw," came the reply from all of the others. "We definitely heard the sound of someone's voice calling to LeRoy."

There was nothing in the area to be seen. The graves all appeared to be intact and nothing had been disturbed.

The night stalking team of young men proceeded down the road to Uncle Frank's cabin. From a distance they could see the jack-o-lanterns lit up and sitting on Frank's porch. They hurried on to his front door and were immediately greeted by their old friend. They told him of their encounter at the cemetery and Frank said that he knew exactly what that was. He also had heard the voice on several occasions in the fall of the year when the night air was quite cold and foreboding. Frank told the boys to come in and sit down by the fireplace and he would tell them all about random eerie occurrences that happened around the haunted cemetery.

Once they were all inside Frank's cabin, they stoked the fire to create more light and they huddled together and prepared to hear more of Uncle Frank's scary tales. Frank lit his pipe, this time with pleasant smelling tobacco, the smoke of which circled his head and filled the room with a pleasing aroma. He took a seat in the large homemade rocker, cocked back and got comfortable, and took a long deep breath.

"Ya see, you young'uns got plenty to learn bouts haints, spirit world, and the like," he said. "I reckon it's 'bout time y'all get a few lessons." Uncle Frank took another deep puff on his pipe and settled back in preparation of telling a creepy story of the spirit world.

The boys' eyes all got big as they huddled closer to each other. As they sat on the floor, they edged closer to the feet of old Uncle Frank.

"Well to start off with," began Frank, "The ghosts and spooks live in a world all their own. Dey got problems of dey own. Sometime, if a spirit is really troubled, he may make himself known to us. Dey don't means no real harm to us, but sometimes we jus' get in dey way."

You could hear a mouse pee it was so quiet in the cottage. No one wanted to move or say anything that would disrupt Frank's story telling.

As Frank continued with his story, he told the lads that he, personally, had several experiences with ghosts. On one occasion, he told the intrigued boys, he was very

167

sick and a ghost came and brought him food and water. At another time, when Frank had just slaughtered a hog, a spirit came out of the hog and chased him for some two miles. The ghost only left him when Frank stumbled over a tree root and knocked himself unconscious. When he awoke the spirit was gone. Uncle Frank then returned to his slaughtered hog and buried it a long distance from his house.

The lads were told that spirits were nothing to get involved with. They might be a blessing to someone, and they may be extremely evil to another. No one can really judge their character.

"All that I ken say is dat ya best steer clear of them altogether," said Frank. "Dey is usually out to do ya harm. Anyone who had delt with a ghost says that he don't want to do it again. I knowed one man who was led into the woods by a ghost. He never came out. When the law went to find him, all dey could locate was his shoes and his clothes. It looked like his body just melted away cause dere was a sticky film all around the area. Dey took dat entire area and made it into the public cemetery, where you stopped tonight."

A chill went up the spine of all of the brave lads. They trembled to think what might have happened had they stayed longer at the gravesites. The old man continued with his explanation of the spirit world. None of his tales were pleasant. It seemed that when a person would seek out a ghost, bad things would happen. If the ghost came to you willingly, it was possible that you would have a more positive experience.

"I would suggest dat you boys don't tarry by the cemetery on your way home tonight." Said Frank. "Even if ya don't see a spook, you may have an encounter with one of the animals that dey keep for helping dem with dey work. The only way to tell if a haunt is nearby is to prick your finger and see if blood or water comes out. If a ghost be around, only water will come out of the prick. If only water is dere, tell yo feet to quickly take you to where you ain't. Yo ken be shure dar is a haint somewhere nearby."

After Frank had gotten the boys completely intrigued, he sat back in his rocker and began to contemplate the lads' earlier experience. The young men could see that Uncle Frank was deep in thought.

"Maybe there be some reason dat LeRoy's grandpa called out for his help," said Frank in a calm but pensive manner. "Maybe the five of us should go back down der and see what we kin find. I'll get a shovel and another lantern. We's headed for another mysterious exploration."

The boys all shuddered at the idea of going back into the cemetery, especially with a shovel. Tommy Jo, being the youngest, suggested that he might stay at the cabin and keep the fire going. Billy Ray, Hank, and LeRoy all were very reluctant, but they didn't want Frank to think that they were scared. They removed their ghost costumes, which they still had on from the night of trick-or-treating. They figured that they could run faster without the costumes, should the occasion arise.

Uncle Frank returned with his shovel and lantern and the four of them headed back down to the graveyard. The young explorers huddled close to Frank as they walked along the dark, dusty road. Soon they reached the gate of the fenced cemetery. It was still open, so the frightened team slowly entered. There was no sign of anything strange or odd going on amongst the several graves.

As they raised their lanterns above the grave of LeRoy's grandfather, they heard a puzzling hissing sound. The sound was coming from within the grave.

"Dare be something down in dere," Frank exclaimed. "Fetch me my shovel. I's g'win' to see what de sound is coming from."

The boys looked at one another as though Frank had completely lost his mind. "Maybe we shouldn't disturb the grave," LeRoy exclaimed. "My grandpappy been resting there for many years. Maybe we should just leave him alone."

Frank agreed with them and they headed back out of the cemetery. When they got back to the gate, they all heard a deep voice calling to them, "Come help me."

Immediately they turned around and went back to LeRoy's grandpa's gravesite. By this time, the three young men were almost paralyzed with fear. Frank just seemed to take it all in stride.

"Give me your pocketknife," Hank said to Billy Ray. "I want to prick my finger and see if I get blood or water."

Uncle Frank said that there was no time for that now. They had to dig quickly.

The dirt from over the grave began to be removed as Frank franticly dug where the hissing sound was coming from. The deeper Frank dug, the louder the hissing and the more frightened the boys became. At about two-feet down, Frank struck something very hard. There was a 'whooshing' sound that came from it when the shovel penetrated its covering. Billy Ray was so frightened that he wet his pants.

"Dat be an ol' water jug," Frank observed. "It mus' have been lef' here by the grave diggers. We done let the air out of it and now maybe dis dead body can get some rest."

Frank then began replacing the dirt which he had removed. The boys all felt extremely relieved when the dirt started to be replaced. No one wanted to dig all the way down to the coffin. Two feet was plenty deep enough.

When Frank had completed filling the grave back up, they all headed back out the gate and down the road to the small cabin. They could see a bright glow coming from the cottage.

"Tommy Jo must have kept the fire going real well," Hank said. "I'll bet he didn't want to get scared by the dark."

"Speaking of scared," exclaimed LeRoy. "He ain't got no idea of the scared that we jus' been through."

The entire group of returning explorers were relieved and happy to be back at the cabin. Uncle Frank flopped down on his wood slat bed and quickly fell asleep. The four youngsters decided that it was time for them to slip out and head back home. Surely their parents would be wondering where they had gone. The boy's spooky exploration story would not be shared with anyone. It would, however, be permanently instilled in all of their minds.

Chapter Eight

Very early one morning, LeRoy was awakened by the clamor of several of the town's people, who were gathered and chatting loudly. He quickly got dressed and went outside to check the commotion. Once outside, he saw that his other three running mates were already there.

A local town lady had been found dead on the road leading into their humble community. She had been mauled with a heavy object and her body had several cut marks. It looked as though she had been clawed by a large wild cat and then dragged into town. What caused the mauling with a heavy object, and what cat would be able to drag a grown woman for any distance? LeRoy could easily see why there was such a clamor and fuss over this strange and puzzling death.

The lady who had been killed, Mrs. Alstead, was a widow who had been living in a small cottage at the edge of town. She had been shrouded with mystery. Many of the ladies in town gossiped wondering how she could afford to live by herself and come to town several times a week to shop and buy groceries. She was always well dressed and often had a new hat and shoes. Her late husband had not been rich and could not have left her with much money to live on. Where did her spending money come from?

The boys looked at each other with a secretive grimace on their faces. They hurried off to a private location so that they could discuss the entire situation. Could it have been possible that Mrs. Alstead had found the Pemberton treasures? Was it the money from those treasures that she was spending so freely?

They decided that the only people that could, or would have, killed Mrs. Alstead were the two scary men who had threatened the boys and had caught them out at the Pemberton estate. The men were mean, and they even cut off part of LeRoy's ear when they were found at Mrs. Pemberton's gravesite. The men had admitted that they had been looking for the Pemberton treasure and wanted the boys to stay away from their search.

Should the boys go to the sheriff with their information, or should they keep it a secret and go try to find the men on their own? Since they had delt with the men earlier, they would have a good chance of tracking them down. Maybe Uncle Frank would help them in their search. If they found the money, they could share it amongst each other. If they found the men, or the men found them, what would they do? The four of them were no match for the two evil men that they were seeking.

The next morning all four of the boys headed off to Uncle Frank's cabin. He was having a cup of coffee and smoking his long-stemmed pipe. They could smell the coffee and the pipe from a mile off.

"He's home," Tommy Jo said. "Let's sneak up on him and take him by surprise."

The boys crept up to the cabin without making a sound. They surrounded the cabin and peaked into the doors and window.

"What y'all up to now?" Uncle Frank called out.
"Come on in and have yourselves some hot coffee. I bees
too relaxed to get up and fix it fer ya."

"How in the world did ya know we was here?"
asked LeRoy. "We been quiet as a church mouse."

"I smelt y'all a coming," said Frank. "Da ain't but
one smell that smells like four boys jus lookin for trouble.
Ya don't think I lives out here not knowing everything that
goes on round me, does ya?"

The boys went in and settled down on the floor of
the cabin. They enjoyed a cup of coffee and all of them
smoked a little rabbit tobacco.

Finally, LeRoy got up the nerve to ask Frank what
they had come for. "Ya know those bad men that was a
tryin' ta find the Pemberton treasure? Well, we think that
they may have killed Mrs. Alstead who lived near town.
She was found all cut up and her head bashed in. Ain't
nobody else who would have done such a thing."

Tommy Jo cut right into the conversation. "Mrs.
Alstead had been spending a bunch of money in town
lately. She had probably found the Pemberton treasure and
was spending it on herself."

"Now you boys slow down some," said Uncle
Frank. "How y'all know dat dis Mrs. Alstead ain't got
some money that her late husband lef' her? And how does
y'all know dat these men had anything to do with her
death? Maybe y'all jus jumpin' off da deep end. Let's all
jus' sit back and ponder all da facts. Den let's ask each

other questions 'bout the situation. Maybe we ken come up with something more factual dan jus guessin' at things."

The boys looked somewhat disappointed because they were ready to go solve the murder mystery immediately. They all sat back with their cups of coffee to contemplate the situation.

"Now what y'all gwin do iffin y'all find them two mean men?" asked Frank. "Is y'all g'win' arrest them by yourself and bring in to the sheriff? Ya gotta think these things out some. Iffin ya don't make plans, den ya might jus' get yourselves in trouble over yo head. I reckon y'all been there before.

"I knows where dem men lives in a cabin deep in the woods," said Uncle Frank. "Let's slip over there one night and see if we can see something suspicious, like them having some treasures. Y'all come over here day after tomorrow and we will snoop around and see what we can see."

The lads were satisfied with Frank's suggestion, so they moseyed back down the dusty lane to their houses.

Time seemed to drag on but finally the day came for them to go and investigate the scary men's cabin. They met Uncle Frank and together they all headed to the secret cabin deep in the woods. As they approached the small house, they saw that there was smoke coming from the chimney but there were no lights on. They cautiously approached the cabin and peeked into one of the two windows. There on the table was a small sack.

"What do you reckon it has in it?" asked LeRoy. "I guess the only way we will know is for one of us to sneak in and take a look."

LeRoy volunteered to slip into the cottage while the others kept lookout for the returning men. When he reached the table, he opened the small cloth bag and poured out a handful of gold coins, gold jewelry, diamonds, and other precious stones. His mouth fell open wide. He had never seen so many precious objects in his entire life. This was more than all the money that he would see in his lifetime. Lifting up the handful of riches and the jewelry bag, he showed it to his fellow explorers.

LeRoy put the riches back into the small bag and placed it on the table. He then went over to the fireplace where he found a single dried paw from a wild bobcat. On this paw, he found dried blood where it had been used to scratch and tear someone's body, such as Mrs. Alstead's. He showed this dried paw to his comrades who were watching through the window.

All of the items were carefully replaced exactly where they had been and LeRoy slipped back out of the cottage. They all headed back to Frank's cabin before the men came back. They wanted to discuss the findings that they had made and what their next step should be.

Back at Uncle Frank's' they all sat around the fire and each one began to tell his feelings. All of them agreed that the two evil men had robbed and killed the widow, Mrs. Alstead. What could now be done about it? Should they report their findings to the law, or should they take it all into their own hands?

Frank pointed out to the boys that they were dealing with a very dangerous and quite fragile situation. If they did turn in their evidence to the sheriff, who would get the treasure? If they went and removed the treasure, who would protect them from the men coming after to get it back. Someone had to come up with a workable plan, and it had to be soon.

The young, makeshift detectives did not want to make any quick or ill-advised decisions, so they all went back to their own homes with the intention of contemplating their next move. Although they didn't want to outright steal the treasure, they were all in agreement that the evil killers of Mrs. Alstead should not have it either. They knew that, in time, the law would catch up to the crooks, but they may have spent the treasure by that time. They all planned to meet back at Uncle Frank's house in two days to discuss their individual plans.

When the time came, they all met back at Uncle Frank's cottage. Everyone had a plan for addressing the problem at hand. Tommy Jo suggested that they break into the men's cabin and beat them to death with shovels. That idea wouldn't work because they would all be guilty of murder also. Hank came up with the next plan. He wanted to burn the men's cottage while they were out. He suggested that first they steal the treasure before the set fire to the shack. This wouldn't work because it would still leave the men to search and find the ones who burned their house and stole their money. LeRoy suggested that they just go to the sheriff and let him take care of the entire situation. That wasn't a bad idea, but who would have the fortune that they had found? Billy Ray came up with the best idea and it was agreed upon by all.

The two men had been setting illegal traps for catching deer and other animals. They would dig a deep pit, place spiked trees at the bottom, cover it up and disguise it. When an unexpecting animal would come along, he would fall into the pit and immediately get killed by the sharp stakes penetrating his body. This was an illegal manner of hunting, but these two lawless men didn't care.

Billy Ray's plan was to go to the men's cabin and steal all of the treasure. They would then wait until the men came home and call to them and let them know that their treasure had been stolen. The men would immediately pursue the boys, who would lead them to one of the men's own illegal traps. The men would fall into the trap and impale themselves on their own sharp trees. This would do away with the crooks, and it seemed to be a proper end for them. The boys would then go back to the men's cabin and secure the dried bobcat's paw. They would then take this evidence to the sheriff and tell him that they had found where the evil men lived. No one had to say anything about the treasure that the boys had found.

When the sheriff went out to the remote cabin of the murderers, he began to look around for other clues. He brought his old blood hound out there to track down where the men had gone. They didn't have to go far before they found the bodies of the two men trapped in their own illegal snare. Both men were dead and it appeared that they had fallen into their own trap. The sheriff removed the bodies and took them back to town, where he announced that the mystery of the death of Mrs. Alstead had been solved.

No one even suspected that there was any treasure, especially from these two deadbeats. No one was even sure that Mrs. Pemberton left any treasure and they certainly didn't know that Mrs. Alstead had found it and hidden it away. The only ones who knew for sure were the two robbers, who were both now dead. Neither the boys, nor Frank, mentioned a word about the treasure. This was their secret and they would take it to their grave.

Back at Uncle Frank's cabin, the group of explorers carefully hid the treasure, coins and jewels by burying it under Frank's cabin floor. They agreed that the bounty was to be shared equally among them, but not until everything calmed down around town. They had to be extremely careful about changing this loot into hard cash because they didn't want anyone snooping around and finding it.

The following year Billy Ray and LeRoy went off to college at the State University. Both of these young men were extremely intelligent and both began their studies of agriculture. LeRoy came up with an ingenious idea. He and Billy Ray would write a book dealing with a better way to grow corn, and other farm vegetables. They would show it to the professors and present it to a publisher. The publisher would then purchase the rights to the book and provide the young men with some usable capitol. In this way, the two students would have some spending money that would keep their hometown folks from becoming curious about where they got the money from.

The plan was put into motion. The book was written, and it was quite a success and sure enough, a publisher wanted to buy the rights to it. The boys returned home with spending money and immediately called a meeting with the other two boys and Uncle Frank. No one knew how much the boys had been paid for their book so no one could question where their money came from.

The five of them would meet at Frank's cottage and share up the money. They would then get some of the gold out of the treasure bag and send it back to the University to be changed back into spending money. LeRoy and Billy Ray continued to do this for several months.

All of the boys shared their money with their parents, who spent it on improving their living conditions. Even Uncle Frank did some fixing up on his old cottage. He put in some fencing and planted a fine garden. When questioned about the source of the money, they all simply said that Billy Ray and LeRoy had shared the money earned from their book. Their parents certainly didn't complain about the extra money.

The four boys had their entire education paid for by selling the treasures. Uncle Frank ended up with a new cabin that had a larger fireplace and several smoking pipes for his fine tobacco. He also bought several acres adjacent to his property and put several of his friends to work gardening and selling their crops in town. Everyone seemed to be happy and content, that is, until they received news of the Great World War breaking out. All four of the boys, who were now men, were called into active duty in the military. Who knew what would be left when they finally returned, or if they would return at all? These were very troubling times, even more so than when the youngsters would sneak off to hear wild tales told by old Uncle Frank.

Chapter Nine

On the following Monday morning, the Army recruiter was at City Hall signing up young men for service in the US Army. Billy Ray and Leroy had been off to college, so they were immediately enlisted with the position of sergeant. Hank and Tommy Jo were enlisted as privates. All of the men, after being processed into the military service, were shipped off to basic training. This training was almost like a game for our four adventurers for they were familiar with crawling through the mud and bushes, as well as avoiding capture by their enemies. Their several experiences with Uncle Frank had served them well when it came to their military training.

When arriving at basic training, all men had their heads shaved and then were given their uniforms and their weapons. The only difference in the men's uniforms was that there were three stripes on Billy Ray's and Leroy's. There were no stripes on the others. The training was the same for them all.

The four hometown friends were very familiar with the use of a rifle. They had all used them when hunting during their younger days. The Army trainers were extremely impressed with their ability to use their rifles, and were more impressed with their accuracy. The "fearsome four" readily adapted to the entire training procedures and soon they were shipped off to active service.

Luckily the four friends were assigned to the same army unit. They were trained for, and sent to, the same military base. There they were instructed as to where and when they would be deployed into action. Actually, they were excited and ready for defending their nation and being a part of putting this entire world skirmish behind them.

LeRoy and Hank were assigned to one company and Billy Ray and Tommy Jo to another. When it came to being deployed into battle, each company went their separate ways. Billy Ray, being a sergeant, was put in command of ten men, one of whom was Tommy Jo. LeRoy and Hank were assigned to a completely different group, with different commanders and different missions.

Hank, being the most courageous of the four country gentlemen, was awarded several prestigious medals for his bravery and for his single-handed capture of twenty enemy soldiers and knocking out six machine gun units. LeRoy and Tommy Jo were awarded the purple heart for having been wounded several times in battle. Billy Ray, being the leader and responsible for the actions of an entire squad, was awarded the meritorious Silver Cross for bravery and superior leadership.

When the war was over, all four brave explorers returned home to their small country town. By this time, the town had grown and was quite a bustling community. The four were heroes in the eyes of all the town residents. They were welcomed home with a parade down Main Street and a special presentation by the mayor. The men's families were all present, as well as the portly, but well dressed, Uncle Frank. Everyone was happy to see one another and they all partook of a large potluck dinner on the lawn of City Hall.

It took several weeks for the returning heroes to meet and greet every resident. Each was eager to hear of the past activities that they had missed. They were especially interested in hearing how Uncle Frank had gone about developing and expanding his agricultural endeavor. He had grown his business into a prosperous enterprise which employed several of his friends and provided a nice livelihood for several families.

The young men were invited to Uncle Frank's new cottage, where they met and gathered around his large fireplace, which was in the living quarters of his multiroom house. They all smoked a little of Frank's special tobacco, and even had a taste of his home-made wine. For old times' sake, as they all gathered around the fire.

Uncle Frank pulled up an old, creaky rocker and said, "You boys set yo'selves ponst one of dem chairs. Pull yo'selves up close. I's g'win' tell you a scary story 'bout a black cat what pounced 'pon its mean owner."

The next hour they all enjoyed listening to old Uncle Frank tell another of his wild and scary tales.

About the Author

Hank Roberts is a retired dentist who spends much of his time with his closest friend and love, his wife of 55 years. He enjoys boating, fishing, traveling, and watching college football.